HEATHER BOYD

Barely a Master

HUNT CLUB – 2

DEDICATION

To the Dream Team – both past and present – who have touched and inspired me through the years. You're always in my thoughts.

By Heather Boyd

Almost an Equal
Barely a Master
Hardly a Stranger

Just a Dream
Never a Gentleman
Once a Husband

CHAPTER ONE

June, 1814

Powder. Shot. Pull the trigger. Just three actions to end the misery.

Aiden Banks, the Duke of Lewes, shifted under the weight of Lady Russell's feminine bulk, too dejected to remove his hand from her large breast. It hadn't been his choice to fondle her. She'd taken the initiative all on her own the moment she'd invaded his study and perched her ample hide on his lap. *Confounding creature.* It never ceased to amaze him she was so blind to his indifference to her reputed charms.

Lady Russell fingered his cravat, a slow crafty smile curving her lips upward in evident satisfaction. "Darling, perhaps we should adjourn to a more fitting location?"

Unfortunately, the deepest parts of hell were all taken.

He dropped his hand so it hung down the side of the chair, so as not to touch her more than he had to. He didn't know what she could possibly want with him. He'd never encouraged her to think him open to her inducements.

Powder. Shot. Pull the trigger.

The refrain grew louder with each passing day.

"I'm expecting company at any moment," Aiden murmured.

"Your heir? How delightful. Robert is a handsome young man, every bit as promising as his father was as a younger man." She moved to touch his head, perhaps to smooth a lock of his hair from his eyes. He escaped her attempt. He didn't like to be touched. "I think we should educate him in the ways of the world. I've never romped with a duke and his heir before. It could be quite . . . stimulating."

Over my dead body. He had firm limits to how far he'd

let his debauchery take him. Lady Russell, on the other hand, did not entertain a scruple of limitation in her being. She liked wide variety in her steady diet of willing men. Young, old, experienced, novice—she wasn't fussed so long as she got her pleasure first. Aiden wouldn't be surprised if she wasn't riddled with disease. The thought made him fidget.

Perhaps he had some obligation, aside from dying and bestowing the title to his late brother's child. He should warn Robert to stay clear of Lady Russell. If she had set her mind on him as her next conquest, Aiden would interfere. The duchy must have healthy heirs.

A bitter laugh welled up inside him, yet he couldn't let it out.

"Stimulation will have to wait for another day," a cross voice grumbled and Aiden almost wept in relief.

He glanced up sharply as his sister-in-law, Mrs. Josephine Banks, stalked into the room like an elemental tempest. Tall, thin and composed of unbendable determination, she'd become the bane of Aiden's existence. His unlikely savior today, however.

"Ah, Mrs. Banks," he replied calmly. "Did you have a good visit to the Royal Academy of Arts?"

Josephine raised one imperious eyebrow at his lack of courtesy. "Never mind that." She glared until Aiden dumped Lady Russell on her own feet and stood as good manners decreed. She inspected him from head to toe and, as he was still properly attired, she faced Lady Russell. "What are you doing here again?"

Lady Russell shook out her skirts, ignoring the venom in Josephine's words. "The duke and I were discussing the possibilities of the future. Nothing that concerns you, my dear."

Although it was hardly ladylike, Josephine folded her arms beneath her meager breasts and scowled at Lady Russell. "The duke's future concerns me very greatly. We are family and with family come certain moral obligations to protect them from adventuresses. He's not for you, and you are certainly not good enough for him. You are attempting to interfere with the course of my brother-in-law's life. That is certainly my concern."

Oh, if only Josephine knew of the pistol hidden from view within his desk drawer. Then he'd see if she cared more for the planned course of his life, or for her son's imminent inheritance. Some days with Josephine it was hard to tell. She was certainly fond of keeping the ladies out of his company.

On some level, he appreciated her meddling. He didn't want to marry, had never intended to marry since he'd once had a brother and now only a nephew to take his place when he grew tired of pretending he liked living. So far, since Josephine had moved into Mercer House, she'd prevented six young ladies from compromising themselves and becoming his duchess. He should thank her one day for that. Perhaps dying swiftly and early would be thanks enough.

But in truth, her enmity towards Lady Russell had nothing to do with the lady's recent habit of gracing his knees. Their hostility stretched back almost two decades to their first Season as combatants on the Marriage Mart.

Never one to take a subtle, or not so subtle, snub to heart, Lady Russell shifted restlessly against his side. Was that meant to be a sensual enticement? The action left him utterly cold. He shuffled his weight to his other foot so they didn't touch anymore.

"Your Grace?"

So much for keeping young Robert and Lady Russell apart. Aiden stepped away from Lady Russell to face his nephew. "Come."

Lady Russell followed him, she stroked Aiden's arm and then gripped his bicep. Could she really be this stupid? He shook off her grip.

"Do you think—?" The boy's words ended abruptly as he took the scene before him. "Forgive me, Your Grace. I didn't realize you had company."

"Lady Russell was just leaving."

Since both Aiden and Josephine spoke the sentiment aloud at the same time, it wasn't surprising that Robert's eyes widened with surprise. He looked suddenly uncomfortable standing there in the doorway.

Aiden took stock of his heir. Tall and weedy, possessed of a sad habit of blushing when he was the center of attention—he feared for the boy's future. Josephine's coddling had ensured he would be easy prey for the most ambitious of the *ton*. Robert needed to learn how to hide his emotions better before he became duke. But that could take years.

Aiden couldn't wait years.

He gestured for Robert to come closer, and then cursed under his breath as Lady Russell glided forward to meet him, smiling as she went. "Mr. Banks, what an unexpected pleasure."

She held her gloved hand out to Robert and he gallantly kissed the air above her knuckles. "Lady Russell," he murmured softly.

Josephine hissed loud enough that Aiden heard, "Little better than a common strumpet."

Lady Russell's back stiffened. She smiled sweetly at Robert and then she took her leave, flouncing out of the chamber with a spring in her step.

"I thought she'd never leave," Josephine muttered, ignoring her son's puzzled expression. She turned to Aiden. "What in God's name were you doing with that woman on your knee? My husband always claimed you had better taste than encouraging an aging harpy with a habit of outliving her husbands. How many has she had now, three?"

"Two. There was never proof of the second." Aiden held his hands out before him, hoping to forestall her tirade. "I hardly encouraged her. She must have bribed the butler again."

When Josephine sniffed her disapproval, Aiden turned for the brandy to ease the pain of her impending lecture. "Really, Lewes, the company you keep. And that Bellow's fellow is the worst bounder. How can you still employ him as a butler? He'd let a street thief into your home."

Aiden tossed down his brandy and refilled the glass. "Nonsense. Bellows terrifies street thieves with merely a look, as does most of my household staff. An essential trait to have when one works for me."

He needed them to keep the world at bay. A pity they failed in Lady Russell's case. She must have used new inducements to get past Bellow. He'd have to increase his pay again to keep her out.

Josephine settled on the edge of a chair, hands elegantly clasped in her lap. "Well, my son and I must live here, too. They have already corrupted my sweet boy into an itinerant gambler. Why, I caught him playing Hazard with your valet last night. I'd thought at least he was honorable."

Aiden rubbed his jaw as he studied his nephew. Robert appeared uneasy. "Did you win?"

A dark blush formed over the boy's face as his mother bore holes into his head with her steely glance. His nephew shook his head. "Almost."

He stepped between them, even though Josephine would likely run her mouth at Robert the minute they were alone again. He was very keen to miss that in its entirety. "Hazard is a devilishly tricky game to win. Few seldom come out ahead. What were you gambling for?"

Robert's cheeks tinted with brighter color. "Cravats, Your Grace."

Aiden turned and regarded his sister-in-law. Her claim of corruption hardly rated a mention, yet she acted as if her son bathed in vice. He supposed he should say something wise, almost fatherly, given his late brother's absence. "Hazard could rob you of the estate long before you inherit a single chair. Keep your wits about you when playing. Bet no more than you carry."

There. That was sufficiently frugal advice to please Josephine, but soft enough not to bruise the boy's pride. Yet, not for the first time, he wished Jared Banks, his younger brother, hadn't left him to provide for his family. What on earth had possessed him to fall off his horse and die from the injuries he'd suffered?

Vastly inconsiderate. But that had been Jared's nature since birth.

Josephine rose to her feet, a pleased grin tugging her lips away from her usually stern expression. "Well, now that is all settled I'll leave you two gentlemen alone. No doubt my son could learn something new about the estate this afternoon, rather than gambling his day away with a mere valet."

Aiden didn't smile in return as Josephine swept out. He sank into his chair and cursed the day he'd foolishly allowed her free with his home.

His nephew frowned at the door. "I wish she would give me a moment's peace." Robert threw himself into a chair, sprawled untidily with his legs over the arms, and covered his face with his hands.

Aiden blinked at the outburst. "She means well."

Robert dropped his hands and stared at him as if he were addled. "Means well? Every time I try to speak with you she's here before me, getting your hackles up by mentioning I should be instructed in how the estate runs. It's positively ghoulish how she mentions my eventual inheritance every day."

Aiden steepled his fingers on the desk, pondering his nephew's startling confession. "Well, you will inherit. She is correct that you have a lot to learn." And little time to do it. However, Josephine would have no idea that he had no plans for a long reign as the Duke of Lewes.

Robert turned fully in the chair. "What I don't understand is why you haven't married one of those women who sigh as you pass. Why, just last week, my dance partner asked all sorts of questions about you. The next night, Mother caught her slipping through the drawing room window." He folded his arms across his chest. "My mother is constantly commenting on everyone else's prospects for marital felicity, except yours. She's even gone so far as to point out who would suit me, and I'll not marry for a bloody long time. I'm barely old enough to be shackled to one woman. Why do you not stop her meddling in your life?"

Somewhere in all that, Aiden supposed he should have provided a response. But the vast outpouring of words stirred his curiosity. Did Josephine truly want her son to gain the title so badly that she dissuaded *all* women from pursuing him? He couldn't be sorry for it. At the moment, their attitudes toward the marriageable misses of society aligned perfectly. Although Josephine's behavior often perplexed him, he shrugged it off. "What did you wish to see me about?"

"I, ah, well—I received an invitation to attend the Hunt Club today. I was hoping you would be willing to accompany me and somehow avoid revealing our destination to my mother."

Aiden's eyebrows rose in surprise at the invitation. He hadn't expected Robert to gain entry to the Hunt Club until he was a few years older. "Staines invited you?"

Robert nodded vigorously as he reached for the letter in his coat pocket. When Aiden saw the tell-tale green sealing wax and insignia pressed upon it, he waved the letter away. He didn't need to see the contents, each invitation was exactly alike.

"He's a friend of yours, isn't he?" Robert hid the invitation quickly, shifting in his chair anxiously. "Your valet said he was a *very* good friend."

Aiden nodded. The Duke of Staines ruled his private gentlemen's club with an iron fist. But that rare invitation to join would set the boy, heir to the Lewes ducal estate and title, firmly among the leaders of the *ton*. He'd have to buy Staines more than one case of brandy in thanks for the unexpected gift. "Tonight?"

"Yes. If you are free, that is." Robert glanced toward the door and moved to the edge of his chair. "Is the invitation for all parts of the house?"

Aiden frowned then realized his valet had been doing more than just gambling with his heir. He'd told him about the secret vice one could indulge in there too.

The man was going to pay for that.

"Staines doesn't offer half invitations." He thought a moment. "I gather you wish for private entertainment as well?" When Robert blushed scarlet, it was Aiden's turn to shift uncomfortably in his chair. "Those types of rendezvous require merely a nod to the major domo on arrival."

"Thank you, Your Grace." Robert jumped to his feet, a wide grin revealing his excitement. "I don't know what I'd do without you."

Although Aiden nodded as Robert went on his way—a jaunty hitch to his step—his dark thoughts crushed him. Very soon his nephew would sink or swim because Aiden couldn't exist in this wasteland man called society. Certainly not for much longer.

He slid the drawer of his desk open and stared at his dueling pistol.

Not yet.

But soon.

CHAPTER TWO

London thrummed with the pulsing vitality of a great beast and Terrance Bridgewater breathed deep the swirling currents of corruption and excessive vice flooding the city. He glanced left and right along the bustling street, content but excited by his return home to familiar surroundings. He'd been buried in respectable countryside far too long.

Now that he had left the vicinity of the coaching house, he patted his coat pocket. It was good to know he hadn't lost his skill at picking the occasional pocket. The cull had had it coming. Five jabs to the ribs with his elbow had not made Terrance warm to him on the long journey from Grantley Park, his last place of employment, to London. But the final indignity was the foul breath that had wafted over him time and again as his seat partner sought to claim even more space on the bench.

He'd come very close to losing his temper, yet he'd hesitated to teach the man his proper place in the world. Perhaps it was the sweet old woman sleeping opposite, or the fresh-faced girl practicing her coy smiles beside her, or maybe it had been the wide-eyed, impressionable youth sitting opposite him that held him back. No one had the right to impose on him. Yet Terrance had hesitated for fear of upsetting the carriage occupants sitting closest.

With a wry grin at his brief moment of soft-heartedness, he tossed the wallet to a grubby-faced urchin. He had no need for the funds contained within. Not now. The sandy-haired boy stared at him, then at the wallet. But every street thief worth his salt knew when life couldn't get any better than having fate smile upon them. The scamp turned tail between two houses and disappeared as fast as his legs could carry him. Terrance smiled, thinking how the lad reminded him of the boy he used to be—desperate and not too proud to beg for hard coin. He'd lived by his wits, and the speed God had given him in order to survive life in the gutters.

Terrance hurried along Mill Street, counting house numbers until he found his destination. Once there, he stopped still to admire the Duke of Byworth's second London residence. Three impressively understated stories, and all at his disposal for the duration of his stay. Again, he experienced a twinge of unease at accepting the duke's generous offer of accommodation. But as Byworth had bluntly put it, Terrance staying here would keep Henry, Terrance's oldest and closest friend, and Byworth's lover, from fretting over his welfare.

The duke's unexpected concern for Henry's feelings had completely thrown Terrance's opinion of their affair to the four winds. Byworth shouldn't care less about his lover's friend after he left his employ, or even during it. But Byworth was adamant about Terrance staying here and had even made him promise to send Henry a regular correspondence—especially when he left England.

Smiling at the adventure to come, Terrance hurried to the front door of number six, Mill Street and rapped the lion-head knocker.

After a long wait, the door creaked open. "Yes?"

He smiled and handed over his letter of introduction to the old butler. "Good afternoon, you must be Finnegan. I have a note here from the Duke of Byworth."

The old man's expression grew worried. "He's not unwell, is he?"

Terrance shuffled on the front step. "The duke is in excellent health, as is everyone from the Park. I've just come from the estate, actually."

Finnegan glanced at the note, and then the baggage at Terrance's feet, lips firming.

He could well understand the older man's dilemma. Byworth had explained the house contained few staff and those here were somewhat aged. If he were an old man, he, too, would hesitate before letting a young, strapping stranger inside. "I'll wait here in the sunshine until you read the note."

The door shut quickly in his face.

At least Byworth had warned him of the quirks of his third household. He'd have to thank him for that. Under normal circumstances, the disrespect would have itched under his skin and ruined his adventure. He wanted to reacquaint himself with London and then head south on a ship. He was bound for the continent as soon as he gathered supplies and booked passage.

Terrance glanced left and right along the street. A neat location, kept in good order and likely to be careful to lock their windows against midnight thieves. He rolled his eyes at his own thoughts. An hour in London and he was ready to slip into his former life as a petty criminal. But he didn't have to steal to survive anymore. He had more than enough funds to support himself for several years of travel, even if he never took on another tutoring position.

Although he'd saved every penny he could, Byworth had slipped him enough funds that even his eyebrows had raised. And all under the condition that he simply write. Terrance had never met another man to be so generous without expecting something in return. Yet the Duke of Byworth had never propositioned him. He had Henry to warm his nights and seemed in no way dissatisfied with the exclusive arrangement.

Luck had finally smiled down upon his friend. Not bad for a pickpocket and former whore.

He peered down the street again as a flicker of movement low to the ground beside a fence caught his eye. But whatever, or whoever, it was disappeared quickly from sight. He frowned. Had his momentary weakness with the bulging wallet and homeless boy set him up to be followed? He didn't particularly care for that outcome.

The door creaked behind his back. "Come in, Mr. Bridgewater. Do excuse my caution. One can never be too careful these days."

Terrance took his hat from his head and stepped through the door. As soon as he glanced around, he clenched the hat tightly at the careless wealth lying around him, begging to be taken. "I'd be worried too." And indeed he was. The house—an ostentatious display that the owner had more money than sense—called to him. He wanted this house and everything in it.

"It's just me and the missus here at the moment. We have a maid-of-all-work come in most days, but her head's full of fever and she's lying abed. Can I take your things?"

He glanced over the older man's frail appearance. "I can manage. If you'd care to show me to a room, I'll get out of your way. I'd not like to make trouble for you."

The butler gave him a queer look. "Wouldn't you like a tour of your house?"

Terrance blinked. "Did you just say 'my' house?"

Finnegan smiled. "We always knew this day would come, sir. It's been many a year since the house had a master in residence. I expect the duke and duchess have settled things between them."

He closed his eyes as a wave of shock swept over him. Now this was unexpected and far too much. Byworth couldn't give away a bloody house, too. The old man must have misunderstood. He held out his hand. "May I see the note?"

The old man shrugged and passed it over.

The bold handwriting glared at him. In two short sentences, Byworth explained the house had a new master—him. As thanks for services rendered, Terrance Bridgewater would reside here for the rest of his life. He closed his eyes. *Bloody wastrel.* It was a good thing Henry had only one close friend. If he had more, his lover would have empty coffers before he'd gained sense.

He had never understood Peers. They had all the money, all the power, yet often stuck their noses, and other parts, in places they shouldn't. Like Lewes.

Terrance gritted his teeth as the image of the Duke of Lewes came unbidden to his mind. He wasn't going to think about that blasted duke for one more minute of his life. "Ah, yes. I'd forgotten all about his generous gift." There was no point having the butler question the situation too closely. Terrance looked about him again. Although Byworth's generosity stunned him, he'd be a fool not to take the house. The place appealed to him immensely.

"Perhaps you'd like a tour now?"

"Of course."

Terrance followed behind the slow moving butler as he was shown his new accommodations. Drawing room, morning room, study, a library that made his fingers itch, a small rear garden that would be pleasant should he step out of doors to read.

Unfortunately, the butler was wheezing as they reached the upper floor. Concerned, but unwilling to show it, Terrance stopped to examine a fine landscape so the butler could have an excuse to catch his breath. "This is very fine."

"Yes, it is. The house boasts quite a few pretty paintings like that," Finnegan gasped. "The duke was always sending things along when the house last had a resident."

Terrance frowned at the second reference to the house's unused state. "When exactly was that?"

Finnegan mopped his brow. "Oh, going on three years now. The duke removed to the country and hasn't returned to London for any length of time since."

Curiosity ate at Terrance. "Did the duke house his mistress here?"

Finnegan stood up straight. "She was a fine lady. Very elegant. We were very sad to see her go."

"Of course."

So the Duke of Byworth had discarded his mistress around the time Terrance and Henry had joined his household and removed them all to the country. He stifled a laugh. What a sentimental fool Byworth was, after all. He'd never delay three years to get the man he wanted in his bed.

Again, Lewes popped into his head. This time he was kneeling before him, hands bound behind his back with ugly iron shackles—dark, unsmiling eyes ever watchful. Terrance grimaced. Lewes had been his most problematic gentleman caller during his time at the Hunt Club. His resistance to being dominated, the very act he paid Terrance handsomely to perform, had made the chore so much harder to carry out.

But some men were never comfortable in their own skin. Lewes' aversion to touch had proved a challenge during the duke's weekly visits. Terrance did not get aroused easily by the use of restraints alone. He preferred eager partners. Partners who wanted to touch him in exchange for the pleasure he offered. Lewes hadn't.

His dark eyes had revealed little of the man beneath the polished exterior, even during sex. Only his groan, ejaculation, and return visit proved he'd enjoyed their time together. The only emotion Terrance had seen him display was fury.

He had yet to meet a man who met his particular needs—none in England, at any rate. Which was why he was so keen to travel, to see new vistas, and to explore new cultures firsthand. To find a man who wanted him and liked him just as he was—with no stage or acting used to entice him to come back.

Terrance shook himself out of his thoughts and hurried after as the butler shuffled off down the hallway.

Finnegan gestured to a room. "This is the main bedchamber. I think you'll be comfortable here."

He walked inside and whistled. The room was perfect and far above what he was used to. Light burst through drapes drawn wide, sparkling off a crystal chandelier hung from the high molded ceiling. A wide, plush bed dominated the center of the room. He could get lost in all that bedding.

Beside him, Finnegan chuckled. "'Tis quite a grand room, is it not?"

"That it is." Terrance hesitated to accept. "But it's particularly feminine. Is there another chamber?"

"None quite so nice. This way."

The butler showed him the remainder of the floor and he was correct. The master suite far outstripped the others with style and comforts. They circled back toward the master suite. He couldn't really pass up the chance to sleep in there. He'd look stupidly foolish in the extreme.

He caught Finnegan's eye. "This will do, after all."

The servant grinned broadly. "I thought you might change your mind, sir. I'll bring your baggage up and unpack for you."

"That won't be necessary. I'll settle myself. I'll not need you to act as valet either."

"As you wish." Finnegan frowned. "Breakfast is usually served at eleven, supper at eight. Is that acceptable?"

"That would be wonderful. No need to change the way things are run on my account." Terrance spun about and hurried down the stairs to retrieve his baggage. There was no point putting the older man into an early grave by running him ragged on his first day.

Besides, this errand would prevent him from inadvertently revealing how much a change in his situation living here was going to be with another incautious remark. He'd hardly ever had the assistance of a servant for his personal needs. Quite likely, he wouldn't know what to request.

He grabbed his burdens and took the stairs two at a time.

Finnegan chuckled, "Aye, to be in me prime again. You seem a fit young man."

Terrance smiled as he strode into his room and deposited his possessions on the bed. "I've always been restless. I cannot wait to be underway again."

Finnegan shuffled further into the room until he stood opposite. "Are you leaving us so soon?"

He flipped open his trunk and removed the first of his clothes carefully. Thanks to Byworth's generosity, he'd be replacing all of them soon. Until he did, he'd care for his possessions as he always had—as if they were his only concern. "I'm traveling to the Continent as soon as I attend to a few personal matters and book passage."

The butler's smile faltered. "You young men, always traveling hither and yon on short trips. We'll be here waiting when you get back?"

"Of course." Terrance didn't correct him as to the length of his trip. If everything went to plan, he wouldn't return at all. He fingered the key in his waistcoat pocket. Damn Lewes and his strange behavior. The key foisted upon his friend Henry, to pass along to him, niggled at his conscience. He'd have to return it somehow before he left England. He didn't like to leave matters unresolved.

He crossed the room, pushing Lewes' key out of his mind, and set his hand to the old man's shoulder. "Why don't you head downstairs? I'll get myself settled in and then come down to the library. I'd like to meet your wife before I do a spot of shopping."

Finnegan didn't smile. "If there's nothing else I can do for you, sir?"

"There's not," Terrance assured him. Yet he was uneasy at dismissing the older man. Finnegan might long to be useful, as Terrance once had. He'd have to relax his control and think of something the butler could do for him.

As the old man shuffled out, Terrance sank onto the bed. Of all the foolish things—getting concerned about an old man's hurt feelings. He shook off the irrational sentimentality and returned to his trunks. It took little time to deposit his clothes into the large oak dresser drawers. He didn't have very much to his name. But he had the Duke of Byworth's cold, hard coin with which to rectify the lack.

Starting this afternoon.

CHAPTER THREE

The vast, cold emptiness of London dragged at Aiden's body. His fellow dukes would laugh to know he hovered on the edge of melancholy, but he lacked the will to care. He was the Duke of Lewes. That name meant something. Once. Perhaps to the last Duke of Lewes, his father. To Aiden it was an anchor pulling him lower, downward to his doom. Suffocating. Smothering him in responsibility and duty. Nothing mattered the way it should. There was no relief for him.

He pulled the curtain aside and peered out onto the London streets. At this time of day, they teemed with gentlemen and pickpockets, ladies and servants. The whores would come later when the blanketing darkness hid their sallow complexions and their gaunt hunger for money at any cost.

He stared restlessly along the footpath. A tall, dark-haired gentleman strolled down the street with a jaunty hitch in his step. He ducked into a bookshop doorway. Despite the great distance, Aiden's first thought was of Archer. He sat up and stared as the carriage drew closer. He caught a glimpse of tousled long black hair, fine fitted clothing and an easy going smile offered up to the ancient proprietor. Archer didn't smile, but even from this distance the resemblance was strong.

The carriage lurched as Aiden reached for the door handle. He curled his fingers into a fist to contain his distress. Three years with no word, with no hint of Archer's whereabouts aside from discovering the other missing whore in service to the Duke of Byworth at his country estate.

Archer wasn't likely to be in London. Aiden had been informed that Archer was as far from him as he could possibly get. He'd failed to acquire any new information regarding the younger man's whereabouts from the Duke of Byworth's servant. He could have pressed, threatened, and hurt the man. But doing so would have angered the Duke of Staines further. Aiden was not so foolish as to offend the closest and most powerful friend he had left. So he'd backed down, albeit reluctantly. Yet the stress of his former lover's absence tortured him. He'd driven the man away as surely as he'd tooled the carriage.

"Is everything all right, Your Grace?"

He glanced at Robert across from him. His late brother's son regarded him with a worried frown. Aiden uncurled his hand and forced his mouth into an apologetic smile for the young man's benefit. "Thought I saw someone I knew once."

"Ah." Robert lapsed into silence.

The trouble with being a duke was that conversation tended to die when he needed it most. He'd never managed the knack for idle conversation and, at times like this, he cursed his stubborn tongue. He could certainly use the distraction as the carriage rumbled along James Street toward the Hunt Club. The last place he'd seen Archer.

Although Aiden would rather be anywhere else than here, he did have a duty to his brother's boy. Today it was to see to his deflowering. The Hunt Club whores would do the deed with little fuss and could be relied upon to be free of disease. The club had strict standards—unlike Lady Russell.

After today's goal had been accomplished, he'd warn Robert away from her with plain facts so as not to leave any doubt about where his best interests might lie. The Hunt Club whores were less trouble until Robert settled on a woman to marry.

His nephew's breath churned as the carriage rolled to a stop. Aiden met his gaze. "Best be quick about it so your mother remains clueless. There will be few in the club at this hour and you may be assured of privacy. Come find me in the Grand Salon when you're done."

With that small encouragement, Aiden stepped out of the carriage and rushed up the steps of the Hunt Club. The exclusive gentleman's club had once been his second home in London, but now each visit was tainted with memories and regrets. He handed off his hat and gloves, and watched Robert do the same while fumbling with his invitation.

Aiden winked at the major domo.

An understanding smile crossed the other man's features and his nephew was led into the bowels of the house.

He turned for the Grand Salon and a much needed distraction. At this hour, the club, all dark wood and leather chairs, was nigh on deserted, but across the room the Duke of Staines sat in conversation with the club's manager. Aiden squared his shoulders and weaved his way through the chairs to join him. Redding, the Duke of Staines' footman, alerted his master to his approach.

Staines ended his conversation and offered a broad smile. "Lewes, good to see you out and about again. I feared I'd have to stage an abduction to remove you from your house and the lovely, Mrs. Banks. Has she taken over the place completely?"

Aiden winced. "Staines, Redding." He'd rather not talk about Josephine now he was free of her scowls. He took a seat, but caught the worried glance exchanged between the two men. The mirror told him he looked as dreadful as he felt, but it pained him that his friend was concerned. Redding retreated a few yards.

Staines leaned forward. "Dine with me tonight?"

Aiden shook his head. "I have my nephew staying with me. He's of a mind to visit Covent Garden later and I cannot, in good conscience, let him go alone. Not until he is a little better acquainted with London."

Staines nodded. "I'd be happy to accompany you, but it's a damn noisy place. Far too many pickpockets and whores for my taste."

"You do remember you run a brothel, don't you?" Aiden frowned.

Staines folded his arms across his chest, but behind him a snort of laughter sounded from his footman. He threw a scowl over his shoulder at Redding. "I run a club for the discerning gentlemen of London, not a low class bawdy house full of lice and disease."

"Of course, Your Grace," Redding intoned seriously, yet Aiden thought the servant was quietly laughing at his master's affront. Redding always had an edge to his words. They sounded respectful, but could easily be not.

Despite the hollow ache in Aiden's chest tonight, a rusty laugh burst free. One of these days Staines would do something about his footman's impertinences. He just wished he could be around to see how the confrontation played out. Would Staines throttle Redding or kiss him senseless? Aiden rather hoped the latter. Redding was a decent sort, for all his poor origins, and Staines deserved a long, happy life. Yet as far as he could tell, Staines and Redding were not lovers. However, there was an intimacy about them that Aiden envied very much.

He patted the back of Staines' hand in sympathy, noting as he did so that Redding's nostrils flared. The footman had hovered behind Staines for so long Aiden was getting very good at reading his moods. He didn't like other men touching his duke. At all. "Of course, you do. Forgive my poorly worded remark."

Redding snorted again, and Aiden had to work at keeping his expression neutral. He'd been a fool to deny himself his friend's company. A few minutes with Staines, and Redding for amusement, brushed his cares away.

Staines turned fully this time. "Did you have something of importance to say?"

Redding shook his head. "No, Your Grace. I have nothing of importance to say at all."

But Aiden rather thought that Redding had a vast quantity of opinion he'd love to share.

Staines rapped his fingertip against the table suddenly. "Well, if you won't dine with me, what brings you to the club at this hour?"

"My nephew is upstairs somewhere."

"Ah." Again, Staines turned toward his footman and, without a word, Redding disappeared from the room. The duke blew out a breath. "That takes care of Redding's infernal hovering. He'll check that your nephew is accommodated properly. Now. What am I going to do about you?"

Aiden raked his hands through his hair. "There is nothing to be done."

Staines sat forward. "Are you lonely? There is a new boy—fresh from the country. Lovely thighs and a firm hand with a whip. He could take your mind off your missing Archer."

His stomach revolted at the notion of submitting to a strange man. He shook his head. "No, thank you."

The other man frowned. "I have it on good authority that Archer's skills were exceptional, but he is not the only man with a flair for dominance in London. Someone else may do very well for you."

Aiden groaned. "You don't understand."

"Then explain it to me," Staines demanded instantly.

A thousand excuses filled his mouth, but not one passed his lips. The truth of the matter was he was lost without Archer's presence. He couldn't find fulfillment with other men. That embarrassment couldn't be uttered aloud. Not even to Staines. The second time it had happened had been more humiliation than he could bear.

Redding rejoined them and whispered into Staines' ear. His friend grinned suddenly. "Enthusiastic. He'll be down later, but he's eyeing a second girl."

Aiden dropped his head to the tabletop to hide the relief that coursed through him. The succession would be assured. The inclinations that had plagued his life would end with him. The duchy would be secure. The next duke would have his own heirs, if the matter was handled swiftly. He'd have to take steps to see Robert wed, despite the boy's protests that he was too young.

And then he would be free.

The thought was distinctly liberating.

"He takes after his father," Aiden murmured. Before his death, his brother had had a string of lovers, beside his wife, who regularly graced his bed. Josephine, poor naive Josephine, had been humiliated beyond a doubt when she learned the truth.

Staines patted his head. "Don't fret. Between us, we'll see that he's courted properly for the duchy's future. There's many a man who would jump at the chance to align their family with the house of Lewes."

Align with Robert, but not with him. That was what Staines did not say. Aiden rolled his head and stared across the room. He met Redding's gaze and sadness smothered his better mood. He had burned too many bridges in the past to be favored by the *ton*. He accepted that. Yet he hated it. He did not belong in London. He never had.

Staines pushed at his shoulder and whispered, "You are rude to be staring at my footman that way. You're not remotely his type."

Aiden set his chin to the tabletop. "Does Redding have a type?"

"Of course he does." Staines bristled, flicking lint from his sleeve.

The gruff set of Redding's features as he closed the gap between them to stand in Staines' shadow choked off his reply. The footman had overheard the conversation, and heard Staines remarks about his type of bed partner. He didn't seem to appreciate being the subject of their talk.

When Redding stopped, Staines turned his head to acknowledge his presence, reaffirming Aiden's belief there was more than a master/servant relationship between them. They were constant companions. Friends almost. Yet neither one of them risked taking things further, despite years of obvious opportunity.

He dropped his gaze to the table as he remembered his own blindness. He'd not known how important Archer was to his existence until the man had disappeared. Was he any wiser than his friend?

Staines sat back suddenly and lifted his hand in greeting. "Ah, you must be Lewes' nephew. Welcome to the Hunt Club, Mr. Banks. I'm Staines."

Aiden turned. His nephew's color was high.

"Thank you for the invitation to the club, Your Grace."

Had the boy's voice grown deeper? He certainly

seemed calmer than his earlier bearing as he conversed with Aiden's oldest friend. Growing into the title of the Duke of Lewes would take time. Aiden had never managed it. Oh, he'd done his duty to the estate and provided for his poorer relatives. And he'd tried to put aside his desires more times than he could count. But he liked a man's firmer touch and not a woman's softness. He could admit his needs freely only now that Archer had gone.

Not for the last time, he wished he might have a second chance to fix things with Archer, to show him he accepted himself. But the man was gone from him and the sad thing was, even if he knew where Archer resided now, he couldn't write or even call out to him. He'd never discovered his real name.

CHAPTER FOUR

As the witching hour approached, Covent Garden was awash with devilry and Terrance soaked up every wicked sensation. He'd been good for far too long. Now that he was back in familiar territory, his fingers itched at every temptation.

A lady strolled on her husband's arm, her reticule carelessly dangling from her wrist. Another couple nearby dripped more jewels upon their persons than could ever possibly be wise. He glanced beyond them and spied a pair of grubby urchins keeping pace with them in the shadows. The foolish pair had been marked as prey.

Terrance stepped aside to let the couple pass, but a tug of guilt tightened his gut that he did not whisper a warning to the lady. She appeared a delicate sort and the eventual confrontation over her jewels would no doubt cause her considerable distress. He shook his head. What happened to them was of no concern. They were nothing to him. Just a pair of cull's fated to pay high for their ostentatious display. Getting involved in other people's business was a sure fire way of getting into trouble.

Further along, he encountered a sight rather more to his taste. A young man waited without apparent purpose at the junction of two paths. Tall, dark haired and with full lips made for kisses, the whore acknowledged his interest by parting his lips and tugging sharply on his waistcoat. When Terrance drew closer, his anticipation vanished. The darkness had hidden the boy's weedy nature and bad skin. He continued on.

He wanted more meat than a scrawny hide could offer. He wanted muscle and heavy bone, full cheeks and a solid cock. He wanted strength held against him. A strong man to match his desire.

Again, the Duke of Lewes flickered through his mind.

Now there was a man who'd had potential but had wasted the opportunity. At his age, Lewes should have accepted his inclinations toward men as a natural need. He had chafed at feeding his hungers. Yet he'd had a body Terrance could put his soul into enjoying and unfortunately missed without a doubt.

He stopped suddenly, hating that the one man who'd come close to satisfying him had lacked commitment, even if Terrance had been the one to leave London. The duke's temper had always been as quick to rise as his cock. Yet it would have been impossible to remain at the Hunt Club after their brawl. And a God awful brawl it had been. Already in a bad mood over a trifling matter with another whore at the club, Terrance had pushed the duke too far, denied him the pleasure he'd expected, and received a trouncing he'd not easily forgotten. Or forgiven.

As soon as he'd been able to draw a full breath without pain, he'd made a serious decision about his future. He'd had enough of pretending to be cruel and breaking in each new man who entered his chambers at the Hunt Club because he was paid well to act the tyrant. Each time a little bit of his soul had withered. Terrance wanted control of his future and, with the small wealth he'd managed to tuck away, he had the means to make a change. Since he'd devoured every newssheet and book that had passed his way, the lure of becoming a tutor had held a surprising appeal.

Then luck had smiled upon his friend, Henry. He'd learned of a country household in need of additional servants, good positions well suited to their skills outside the bedchamber, and he suggested leaving the Hunt Club together. Terrance had jumped at the chance to join an estate far away from London. Despite their inexperience, he and Henry had gotten the positions and they'd left Town for what he'd hoped to be more interesting parts for the country.

But the change of scenery hadn't really suited his temperament. He'd grown bored too soon and found nothing to tempt his inner desires. Which was half the reason why he'd come to Covent Garden tonight before heading off into parts unknown. He was eager to find someone anonymous to take the edge off his desires.

He followed along behind a crowd of revelers. A man alone was often a target for the harder class of thieves. For the time being, some caution was called for. He had no desire to test his skills at self-defense just yet.

The crowd stopped and met with acquaintances. Terrance envied them their large circle. He knew no one here he cared to acknowledge. But he saw Meg, the flower seller from Arlington Street, supplementing her income with a gentleman customer. She hooked her arm through her beau's and disappeared down a dark walk. When Terrance turned back, his adopted group had moved on without him. He stood alone.

He chuckled. *How dare they?*

He set off at a leisurely pace, and came upon another group milling about. The company was all men, all finely dressed and although he intended to pass them by, their conversation intrigued him. There seemed to be a genuine sense of companionship among them. One laughed aloud and the sound stopped Terrance in his tracks.

The Duke of Staines.

Terrance cursed under his breath. Another man turned his head and his panic doubled. Redding—the duke's and the Hunt Club's problem solver. Redding took two steps from his group and Terrance took the same away, the movement akin to dancing. Yet Terrance was engaged in a battle of wills. It just depended on whether Redding would leave the duke's side and come after him.

A young man turned to see what Staines and Redding stared at, and the shock of him stilled Terrance's heart. A younger version of Lewes stared back. Thinner, darker hair, but an almost exact copy. And then the real man stepped from his shadow.

Time halted.

"Archer?" Lewes whispered.

The shock of seeing Lewes in the flesh stopped his heart completely. His lover's cheeks had grown sharper, yet his outward appearance was unchanged. He still wore the tight fitting coat that required assistance to remove. But he would know that face, and the obscenely large diamond cravat pin, anywhere. Like a ghost rising from the cracked ground, the duke approached, bringing a rising tide of need with him.

Terrance shook his head. No. He'd not go back to the way things had been. He had his freedom now, and more control of his life than he had ever known. He spun about and strode into the darkness, little caring where his steps took him. He knew Covent Garden like the back of his hand and he quickly put considerable distance between him and the duke's party.

Yet he was followed. He could hear the rough pant of a man pursuing him with little regard for his safety or his consequence. Irritated, Terrance ducked behind a wall and the man barreled past his hiding place.

Lewes. And alone. The damn fool. He'd get his throat slit for the blasted diamond pin in his cravat.

Despite his better judgment, Terrance followed him, and just in time too. Lewes was stopped by a pair of barrel-necked bruisers twice his size. Although impressed that Lewes didn't turn tail and attempt escape, Terrance couldn't allow him to be hurt if he could prevent it.

He stepped up beside his former lover. "Gentlemen, there are easier pickings farther along," he drawled.

The rough pair exchanged glances. Their postures tensed, prepared for battle. They rushed him. Terrance pushed Lewes out of harm's way, landed a solid punch to one, and lodged his knee into the gut of the second. The first thug swung a fist and Terrance caught it, twisted his arm until the man screamed in pain and fell to his knees. Terrance released him, set his foot to his rump and shoved hard. The man slammed to the ground and moaned.

The second man stood with his fists raised before him while gasping for breath. *An amateur boxer?* Terrance smiled. He knew how to deal with his kind. If nothing else, his childhood on London's streets had taught him how to win. Speed. He stalked in quickly and struck a quick jab to his face. Ugly number two crumpled to the ground without delivering a blow.

Terrance turned, snagged the Duke of Lewes by the arm and hauled him back toward his party. The idiot's face was slack with shock. "Fool. Do you have no sense left in you? The Garden is no place to walk alone."

They had covered perhaps twenty paces before Lewes dug his heels into the earth. An odd gleam lighted his usually barren expression. "I wasn't alone. I was with you," he blurted. "Where did you learn to fight like that?"

Wonderful. This was what he hadn't counted on. But he had little interest in Lewes' attempt at conversation. Debating pugilism had no value to him. "Nowhere you'd want to hear about. Staines is in that direction. I suggest you rejoin his party without delay before someone else decides they want what you have." He flicked the duke's cravat pin to remind him of its value and turned to go.

But Lewes held firm to his arm. "Wait. Where have you been? Where are you staying?"

Terrance shook off the grip and ignored the questions. "Go back to Staines."

Determined to avoid further conversation, Terrance stalked off into the darkness. But before he'd gone too many paces, Lewes fell into step beside him.

Of all the idiotic things to do. A duke did not keep company with a male whore in public. Did Lewes want to be seen and risk his neck? He pulled Lewes into a secluded spot and shoved him hard against a brick wall.

Lewes gasped—the sound reminiscent of his weekly visits to the Hunt Club's torture room. The reminder soured Terrance's remaining enjoyment of the evening. "Damn it all. Must I spell out the situation using small words for you to understand? I am no longer a man whose attentions can be engaged for fifty pounds a night. I've not returned to whoring."

The duke heaved a heavy sigh. "That is the best news I've heard since you left me without an explanation."

He drew back. "Why would you care whether I informed you or not? Many men at the Hunt Club would do the job you want. I'm sure they found someone the next night to master you."

Lewes leaned closer. "Our association was never as simple as that. You gave the orders and I followed. The last thing you said to me was get out. And I did it without question because you wished it, even though I wanted to remain and make amends for my outburst. What was I supposed to do after you disappeared?"

Terrance crossed his arms over his chest, but Lewes' question distressed him. "You never, ever followed my instructions to the letter."

The other man lowered his head. "I should have. I will do whatever you ask so long as you don't send me away again."

Terrance raked his hands through his hair and tugged. He'd not expected his instructions to take, but it seemed Lewes might have accepted them at face value and assumed he'd enjoyed what they'd done together. What would Lewes say when he learned it was all an act? "Can you not get it through your thick skull that we are done with each other?"

Lewes' gaze rose, but he kept his face averted. A submissive gesture of obedience he'd never offered before. Arousal roared through Terrance, mocking his belief that he could forget this man. His cock thickened, his fingers tingled with the need to push Lewes to his knees and brush the tip across his mouth. But the duke would undoubtedly fight that kind of pleasure. He had before.

Lewes lifted his chin, and for the first time Terrance glimpsed more than just a flicker of emotion in his gaze. The duke was desolate. "If you are done with me, then my soul is lost. You've ruined me for anyone else. I belong to you. I want the same as you."

His heart jumped to his throat. "You would demand pain. I do not, that is to say, I was paid to inflict that upon my clients. I don't want to hurt anyone anymore."

Lewes shook his head. "I have pain now and I don't care for it. Your way will suit me. Just give me another chance."

"Were you always this stubborn?" Terrance growled. "If I had my way now you would be on your knees already with my cock between your lips."

CHAPTER FIVE

This time the bluntly worded command did not disgust Aiden. This time his cock thickened with the knowledge that he could have Archer back in his life if he complied. He dropped to his knees, lips parting on a sigh.

Pain lanced his skull as Archer pulled him to his feet by his hair.

"Have you lost your mind?"

"Isn't that what you want?"

Archer shook him. "There is a time and place for such matters. Do you want to see us both dance upon the gallows?"

Aiden glanced left and right. "We are alone. No one can see us."

"You are as foolish as before, Your Grace. You haven't learned a bloody thing. Run back to Staines and make good use of the privacy afforded by the club for your pleasures."

His stomach dropped to the soles of his bright polished boots. "Please," he whispered, "I cannot go back to that."

Archer's scowl grew, but Aiden wouldn't retract the words. Too much of his contentment rested on the other man's broad shoulders. Three years ago, he hadn't understood what he'd had, what he needed. He couldn't lose him again.

Archer's weight shifted from foot to foot, restless and wary. Aiden couldn't blame him. He needed a good reason to stay. "Did you get the key I sent through Arrow?"

A weary sigh passed through the younger man's lips and he stepped away. "Eventually."

He followed, anxious that his quarry not disappear before they'd talked. "The contents remain locked, and I haven't touched them or visited the Hunt Club's upper rooms since you left. Please, stay with me."

"Really." Archer stepped closer, nostrils flaring in a way Aiden remembered and had missed. "Then I gather you're about to go off half-cocked?"

"No, sir. I am prepared and able to wait for your command."

Archer leaned closer still. "Now, that is a valuable trait in a man."

When he remained close against Aiden, hope and anticipation soared in his breast, but he suppressed his physical reaction and exercised the restraint he'd lacked before. Before, he would have rushed, eager to get what he wanted and leave again. And Archer hadn't liked loosening the reins—he'd preferred his own slower pace.

Archer moved away. He stopped a few steps from Aiden and looked at him from over his shoulder. "Come along, Your Grace. The night is passing."

He shuddered at the invitation. He quickly reached Archer's side and forced his steps to slow as they strolled from Covent Garden as if they were simply friends out for an evening of entertainment. Aiden liked the thought of that. He'd never spent time with Archer outside the walls of the Hunt Club. The excitement of it woke his soul.

Archer hailed a hack and ushered Aiden inside, before he gave the directions for a nearby street to the driver. The carriage rocked as he sat opposite. His dark form dominated the space as they got underway, just as he had when they were alone at the club. "Was the entertainment at the gardens to your taste, Your Grace?"

Aiden licked his lips. "Tolerably good." He shrugged, aiming to hide his excitement. "I think the band of jugglers should practice more."

Although the carriage was dark, streetlamps revealed that the corner of Archer's mouth turned up in an amused smile. "Are you an expert in juggling?"

The question flummoxed him. Why were they making small talk? Why had Archer not dragged him to his knees for the journey and imposed his will upon him. "No."

Archer set a booted foot beside Aiden's thigh and rested his wrist on his knee. The widened stance, the command with which he held his attention, brought a lump to his throat. He had missed—

"There really is some skill to it. I've tried it a time or two, but sadly dropped the pins on my head. There is an art to it, all right, as there is with most acting. Like dressing the part of a duke, but not really feeling good enough to be one. I imagine that would take a lot of practice. A man's whole life, perhaps."

Aiden gasped. Had Archer turned clairvoyant in his absence, or had he always been this astute? How could he know that holding the title of duke had always fitted ill with him? And that he'd always felt ashamed of feeling that way about his heritage. He licked his lips. "You may be correct."

Archer's brow rose. "Go on."

Talking about his feelings had never come easy, and here he was, within reach of his lover and forced to talk. He gulped. He had to comply with Archer's wishes or he would disappear again. "It is a lonely life for a gentleman not prone to talk. My parents and brother spoke enough that I never considered my silence until I inherited. It still seems odd that people look to me for an opinion. Makes me cross."

Archer smiled ruefully. "Yet you have learned to impose your will upon others in often quite brutal ways. Has that made you feel like the duke you should be?"

"No." Fear crawled around Aiden's belly. Would Archer turn him aside following that confession?

"As I thought." The younger man dropped his foot and leaned forward. "I never enjoyed acting in the role required of me at the club either. But you do what is required unless you want to be turned out. We make sacrifices to please others."

He gulped at the idea that Archer hadn't enjoyed being with him at the club. For Aiden, the minute he'd left Archer, he had thought of little else 'till his next visit.

The carriage rolled to a stop. When Archer reached for the handle, Aiden lurched toward the door to prevent his escape. Archer stilled him with a light touch to his wrist. "Be calm, Aiden. We've reached our destination."

Shock held him still. It had been a long time since he'd been called by his first name. Hearing it pass Archer's lips sent a thrill racing through him. His cock thickened beyond his power to control, but he had to hide his reaction. He thought of Lady Russell's ample breast in his hand and found control once more.

Archer's brow rose at the sound he must have made, but then he stepped out, leaving Aiden to follow or not. He threw a bright coin to the driver.

When Aiden joined him, Archer was scowling into the distance. He looked around. The quiet street was completely at odds to where he expected to be.

Their fingertips brushed and, startled, Aiden jerked his hand to his chest.

Archer frowned at him, then he ushered Aiden from the street. "Say nothing when we enter."

"Where are we?"

The other man scowled. "My London home."

Aiden blinked. Archer had a home in London? How was that possible? Stunned, he quickly followed his lover up the tidy front steps and waited as he inserted a key into the lock. When the door pushed open silently he stepped into more opulence than he dreamed possible in the home of a former whore. He clenched his jaw shut quickly, lest Archer see and take offense.

"Up the stairs, first on the right and quietly," Archer whispered in his ear.

Aiden hurried to do his bidding. But when he got to the top, he lingered and heard Archer speaking to another man. A servant, perhaps?

He didn't have long to consider it as Archer's heavy tread climbed the stairs toward him. He spun about and stepped into darkness. A shiver of anticipation stroked his back as Archer closed the door with a soft click.

"The butler is too old to climb the stairs with ease and seems hard of hearing. He never noticed your arrival."

Aiden turned. "As you wish."

"I do." Archer shrugged out of his coat. "No point upsetting the apple cart and shocking the poor man into an early grave. I'll see you out first thing so Finnegan doesn't notice you."

He nodded in the dark, but his eyes had adjusted to the faint light by now. Moonlight shimmered upon glass. "Seems a good place to live."

"You mean it's richer than I deserve?" Archer snorted. "You are correct, of course. A whore doesn't belong among crystal and rich silks."

"It is not that. It is just—" Aiden couldn't finish his thought. He'd never considered what kind of place Archer had come from or where he'd gone to.

The other man approached. "What?"

"I didn't know where you'd live. I thought somewhere more—"

"Masculine?" His teeth flashed white in the darkness.

Aiden forced his hands to relax at his sides. "Yes."

A grin curled Archer's mouth. "So did I, but that bed is heavenly. Do you need help with your coat still?"

Aiden swallowed. "Yes."

Archer twirled his finger around in a circle and Aiden turned as if he'd been spun. His tight coat sleeves were tugged over his hands and then whisked away. "A man should be able to undress himself," Archer whispered in his ear. His warm breath sent a thrill through Aiden and he rotated.

Archer stood before him. He slowly pressed a hand to the center of Aiden's chest and pushed. When his back hit the bed post, the man held him there.

His breath hitched tight in his chest at the realization they were alone once more. He had a chance to make things right this time, to fix the mistakes he'd made before. Yet he didn't know the first thing about what Archer wanted. He'd said his behavior before was all an act. What did he really want now?

He held still as Archer explored his chest with a soft touch. Usually, his lover waited until they were joined together, when he couldn't respond to the caress because his hands were bound. But there were no bindings today, only Archer's warm hands stroking his sides. This time the caress didn't trouble him. It was Archer's way. The gentle touch, however, sped his arousal.

"Archer," he hissed.

His lover drew back, wariness replacing the friendliness of his earlier gaze. "That name is dead and gone."

He nodded quickly. "By what name shall I call you, then?"

Terrance recoiled. Did Aiden really not know his name?

What a fool he was. He could have saved himself the trouble of withholding his name in so many situations if he'd realized that simple truth. He could remain anonymous still by giving a false name to the duke now, but as he looked into Aiden's face, dark eyes pleading for the truth, his tongue betrayed him. "Terrance Bridgewater."

The first smile he could remember ever seeing on Aiden's face startled him.

"Terrance," Aiden whispered, blinking rapidly as his hands fluttered at his sides.

With one hand pressing Aiden against the bedpost, Terrance leaned forward and brushed his lips lightly across his lover's.

The duke's eyes widened in surprise, his hands curled into fists.

Kissing had never been part of their past relationship, yet Terrance enjoyed it very much. Aiden would have to get used to it or leave. Still holding him in place, he brought his face closer and then licked over those slack, startled lips. Aiden swallowed—a nervous gesture that hinted he had no idea how to react.

Terrance inched closer until their cocks touched through their clothes. That seemed more to Aiden's liking as a moan escaped his lips. But Terrance was not done with kisses. He had a duke's mouth to explore. He ran his tongue along the seam of his lips as Aiden pressed his hips hard against him. He pushed against that wide, firm chest he loved to touch and licked at his mouth again.

A harried groan passed Aiden's lips. "Please."

"Quiet. Open your mouth for me," Terrance commanded.

Those tempting lips parted and Terrance leaned forward. At the first proper touch, Aiden whimpered. Terrance curled his hand around his lover's skull to hold him steady. He wanted kisses with his pleasure tonight. He wouldn't settle for anything less. He was done playing the part of a disinterested tyrant. He wanted something much gentler than that.

The second kiss was better received, yet still chaste by his standards.

By the time the night was through, however, Aiden would know his kiss and demand it for his own. If he did not, they truly were through. And Terrance may very well regret it. Already he was hard with want. He resisted the urge to turn Aiden around and ground the head of his cock against his hole, ready or not.

Yet he would never force himself on another man. He'd been buggered too often with too little care to inflict that on anyone else. He kissed Aiden again, making a tentative sweep across his open lips as he did so and received another shuddering gasp in return.

Yet it was not disgust. Aiden's cock strained in his trousers. His lover simply did not know how to react to his tenderness. Terrance hauled the duke hard against him and nipped his jaw. "Put your arms about me. Touch me in return."

His lover's embrace was tentative at first. But when Terrance attempted another kiss, sweeping his tongue inside Aiden's mouth, their exchange became frantic. He allowed the frenzy for a little while, quite pleased to have ruffled Aiden's composure, but he soon soothed him. "There is no rush tonight, no one waiting for the room, or spying to see what we do. There are hours 'till daybreak."

Aiden gulped in air loudly against his shoulder and he rocked his lover gently in his arms. Patience had never been Terrance's strong suit either, but after three years of deprivation he had some serious exploring to do. He would do everything with Aiden that whoring at the Hunt

Club had denied him. He would make love to Aiden the way he chose.

He pushed away and reached for the fastenings of his clothes. Tonight there would be no games, no masks, not props to set the stage. Tonight he'd find out if Aiden could enjoy sharing a bed with him.

Once he'd divested himself of all but his trousers, Terrance turned around. Aiden hadn't moved, hadn't stripped one piece of clothing from his body. The sight didn't please him. "Have you changed your mind, Your Grace?"

Aiden shook his head. His mouth moved, but no words came out.

Terrance drew closer. "What then?"

The duke lifted a hand and he settled the tips of his fingers against Terrance's bare skin. "I thought I'd never see you again. I thought I had ruined everything."

The tentative touch was like fire in his veins. "You never had me of my own free will. I was bought to service you, remember?"

Aiden gulped. "And tonight?"

"Tonight is because I wish it. As I wish it, too."

A ghost of a smile crossed Aiden's lips so Terrance kissed him, and ended up stripping the duke himself. Damned foolishness to expect other men to take off your clothes and having no inclination to do it yourself.

When Aiden was bare, Terrance pushed him onto the bed, finished undressing and joined him.

CHAPTER SIX

Aiden had thought he'd found Archer, but this man, Terrance, was a stranger to him. He might look like the handsome devil who'd given him pleasure while he'd been bound hand and foot to the posts of a massive four poster bed, but they were so different in nature. Had everything between them, everything he'd thought he'd had in the Hunt Club, been an act?

Terrance's kisses were strange. Raw. Arousing. They had never been intimate this way before. Not face to face, or on a soft bed. When he thought about it, they'd barely touched. Or rather, Aiden hadn't been in a position to do so.

His lover's hands were everywhere, holding them close while they kissed. His fat, papery soft cock slid against Aiden's, teasing him with the promise of more to come. Yet it would be different tonight, and part of him was afraid of what that difference might reveal.

He twitched the long soft strands of Terrance's hair away as they tickled his ear. His lover moaned, rubbing his cock harder against Aiden's. His voice remained familiar. Terrance's deep growls and moans still swept him with delicious shudders at the ragged need they contained.

Everything changes. Perhaps this way might be better.

He set a hand on Terrance's lower back and marveled in the heat of his skin. Tight muscle shifted, smooth skin slid under his palm as the heavy weight hovering over him pressed closer. Aiden followed the other man as he rolled until they lay side by side. He rested his head on the tight muscle of his arm and set his hands to the broad, unfamiliar, vital chest heaving before him.

Aiden drew back, staring at the man who had shaken his world completely.

Terrance met his gaze and held it as he closed one

hand over his arse. A moan slipped past Aiden's control as his fingertips delved along his cheeks. Terrance brushed over the crease with excruciating softness, teasing as he had never done before. He liked the teasing. It made his cock throb impatiently.

He slung one leg over Terrance's wider thighs and gave him better access.

The younger man shifted again, closer, as his fingertip brushed across Aiden's hole. "I want you. More than I thought possible," he whispered.

Aiden shuddered as the tip of Terrance's finger pushed inside him. The slow fingering took his breath away. He kissed Terrance, forcing his tongue inside his mouth to mimic the pace he wanted. But his lover kept up the same slow penetration; denying him the swift end he craved.

He writhed on that finger—tense, impatient, and desperate for something far larger. He ran his hands over Terrance's chest, remembering everything he'd had done to him while bound. He brushed his fingers over the tight peaks of Terrance's nipples and then plucked one.

When Terrance groaned, he did it again, and again—pulling harder on his flesh until his lover thrust harder into him. Terrance added another finger, stretching Aiden until it was almost enough. He nipped and kissed Aiden's neck, sending exquisite thrills along his spine.

Aiden would explode in an embarrassing rush if this went on much longer. His cock ached for release, his seed leaked from the tip and painted Terrance's belly. His arse begged for more than mere fingers. "Please," he whispered, and then he sucked hard on his lover's lower lip.

Terrance withdrew his fingers and he flipped Aiden over onto his stomach. The bed rocked and then everything from his past and present coalesced as blistering hot skin pressed against his bottom.

Terrance probed with the head of his cock, and then drew away. Cold liquid, likely oil, drizzled over the base of Aiden's spine, sliding into his crease and coating his hole. He shuddered as Terrance's fingertips penetrated him again with greater ease, slicking his entrance with fast, hard thrusts.

The fingers withdrew and then . . . Terrance's thick cock pressed against him, sliding slowly into his resisting body until they were joined.

The relief brought moisture to his eyes and he wiped the sign of weakness away. But as Terrance slid in and out, his body betrayed him. He shuddered and shook in the grips of joy. This was what he'd loved and missed— this moment when he was part of someone else. Part of Terrance Bridgewater. The former whore who made him feel wanted—even when he caused pain.

He took deep, even breaths as the thrusts became harder, faster, and as deep as possible. He loved this. He loved Terrance fucking him. Aiden froze. He couldn't find his breath as that thought led to another.

Terrance dragged him upright, onto his knees, as his pounding took away Aiden's absurd thought. His cock swung, stiff and ignored by both of them, so he took himself in hand and beat in time with his lover's thrusts.

Too soon, the peak crested over him. He shouted as ropes of seed coated the bed.

Behind him, Terrance stiffened and pumped up, up— always up—as he found his release too.

Aiden set his hands to the bed and hung his head, astounded by how different their coupling had been tonight. He had enjoyed that more than he thought possible. And there had been no real discomfort to heal from—just Terrance fucking his arse witless.

As his lover withdrew, Aiden sought to find his place in the world again. He wanted more. He wanted this every night. Yet as Terrance cleansed himself and then Aiden of the oil, he couldn't quite put those thoughts into words. He was afraid of revealing how much he needed this man in his life.

He'd been taught to guard his heart and show only indifference.

As Terrance pulled him under the covers gently he was still tongue-tied. And when Terrance curled up against his back, his arm stealing around Aiden's waist, his lips brushing over the top of his spine, he put off saying anything at all.

It was strange to be held by another when passion had passed, but he did not mind it so much tonight. It was comforting to know that he'd satisfied Terrance. That he'd done something correct for a change.

Within a minute, his lover's snore sounded through the room—leaving Aiden alone with his tumbling thoughts. He set a hand beneath his cheek and closed his eyes and prayed he wouldn't wake to find it all a dream.

Terrance was in serious trouble.

He did not want to toss Aiden from his bed, but he had to wake him soon and get him out of the house unobserved. He had dressed himself in silence already, but he was reluctant to disturb his sleeping lover when he appeared so peaceful. Yet he couldn't keep him like this. The duke had a reputation to protect and responsibilities elsewhere. Terrance had no place in his life past last night.

He set a hand to the sleeping man's chest, marveling at the night that had passed. He'd enjoyed fucking Aiden again. He'd enjoyed touching him very much.

And Aiden had touched him back.

There were no words to describe how his heart had leaped when his lover returned his attentions in equal measure. It had made the end of their association less bitter. Less disappointing. Knowing that he had been desired by the duke outside the Hunt Club's strict confines had soothed his battered ego considerably.

But last night was a farewell, not a new beginning for them.

Once Aiden returned to his world, and Terrance boarded ship, they would likely forget all about each other. At least now Terrance would not feel so much regret. Now he would have fonder memories to cherish at night.

He shook the duke. "Time to go before the sun rises, Your Grace."

Aiden sat up suddenly, his chest heaving.

Terrance smiled, smoothing a hand over the duke's back to calm him. "I'll help you dress." He stood and collected the duke's garments—fine clothes, but too fussy for his taste.

The duke scrambled from the bed in a rush and consented to being dressed in silence. A lump formed in Terrance's throat at how helpless Aiden often appeared. Yet he was a powerful man—a wealthy duke with more than enough servants to cater to his needs. All bar the need Terrance fulfilled, that was.

He turned the duke to face the mirror, curled his arms about his shoulders, and tied his cravat the way he remembered he liked. "There now, perfect once more."

"Hardly perfect, but it will do." Aiden smiled ruefully. "Never have been a perfect duke."

Terrance cupped a hand around the duke's jaw and peered deeply into his dark eyes for the last time. "And I make a poor showing myself. Barely good enough to be any man's master."

Aiden lurched forward and kissed him suddenly, tongue invading and tasting his depths. He drew back just as swiftly. "Good enough to be mine. Clever enough to fool me into believing you enjoyed our time together. It is hard to admit, but I missed you."

Terrance drew back in surprise. He hadn't missed Aiden's company, except for the thrill of fucking him. He doubted the man wanted to hear that, though. He reached for Aiden's fine coat, shook the fabric so it snapped, and held it out.

When the duke was dressed impeccably enough to walk along London's streets, Terrance gestured to the door. They crept from the house, walked along the quiet streets in silence, and only stopped when Aiden's house came into view. This was as close to a particular Mayfair residence as Terrance could ever bear to be. He glanced in that direction and then shook off his sudden anger.

The duke turned. "Can I see you again tonight?"

Terrance rocked on his heels, considering. He did want to see Aiden again, but what were the chances were of Finnegan missing Aiden's presence for a second night in a row? It was too great a risk. He licked his lips, prepared to say no.

"Damn it." Aiden swore. "Not tonight. I'm expected to attend the Henderson Ball. Josephine will make my life a misery if I decline at the last minute."

His heart thumped hard at those two names. He'd only ask about one. "Josephine? I hadn't realized you'd married, Your Grace. Good evening then." He turned on his heel, prepared to sprint from his disappointment. The one thing he hated was married men who dabbled with him on the side. He had no time for them.

Aiden caught his arm in a tight grip. "My sister-in-law, my late brother's wife, lives with me now. She's slowly driving me insane with her meddling, but I promised to attend."

The tight bands squeezing Terrance's chest eased a little, yet he was alarmed by how upset he'd become over a mere woman—a woman that Aiden cared enough about to not want to break a promise. She must be dear to him. She was family, where Terrance was nothing more to him than someone to fuck.

He removed the hand still clutching his arm. "Then I wish you a pleasant evening, Your Grace. However, I am otherwise engaged for the next night. Farewell."

With that, Terrance rushed away, alarmed that he missed the duke already.

CHAPTER SEVEN

The depressing clip of feminine footsteps and swishing silk crossed Aiden's study and paused before his desk. He didn't look up from his calculations immediately, not when he was close to completing the vexing task. With evening approaching, he was eager to finish and turn his mind to more interesting matters. He'd been slowed down by Robert's incessant but perceptive questions all day long and what should have taken half a day had swallowed the whole of one.

Any other day and he'd have sent Robert from him long ago. Educating his heir required a level of patience Aiden usually lacked. Today, however, his mood better suited the endeavor.

In the end, Josephine cleared her throat to get his attention. "Where were you last night?"

Aiden looked up from the estate reports and gave Josephine his best scowl for her interruption. "Not that it is any of your business, Mrs. Banks, but I was out with friends."

He focused on the papers before him as the memory of Terrance Bridgewater caused a rush of heat to his groin. He thickened at the memory and had to use the thought of Lady Russell's ample bosom again to diminish his desire.

As if sensing his mind had turned to scandalous territory, Josephine scrutinized him from head to toe. After a long moment, her gaze softened marginally. "You must have enjoyed yourself. I haven't seen you smile so in years."

Aiden wiped a hand across his mouth to hide the delicious warmth that trickled through him at the reminder of last night. Not even the prospect of tonight's ball was enough to dampen his high spirits. He'd found Archer, or rather Terrance Bridgewater. The victory was as heady as last night's pleasures had been.

Yet Josephine and Robert had to remain absolutely ignorant of that part of his life. He ignored her curiosity. "Did you want something?"

Josephine bit her lip, an unexpected and nervous gesture he'd thought her incapable of making. He dropped the pen to the desk and gave her his full attention. Something was surely wrong. Her gaze cut to her son and back. "I was wondering about tonight."

The ball again? Aiden rolled his eyes at her single-mindedness. "You expect to arrive at eleven. The best looking carriage and grooms in attendance. The Duke of Lewes and his heir decked out in elegant frippery. Is that correct?"

She bit her lips again, eyes straying to her son once more. "Yes, but . . . if you have made other plans for your evening then I can offer your apologies to the Henderson's. I am sure they will understand."

Puzzled, Aiden regarded his sister-in-law. She was awfully keen to offer him a reprieve from the festivities, if launching a debutant could be considered festive at all. What the devil was she up to now? "Robert and I have matters to complete here, and then we're off to my club to dine. We will return in time to change and escort you out. Never fear, Mrs. Banks. We will make a splash of it, as you wish."

Again, she worried at her lip. "So, you are going to the club? You've barely ventured there over the past few years."

He cursed under his breath. Josephine really did pay too much attention to his private affairs. Attending the club had, in fact, lost its appeal the minute Terrance had left London. Perhaps he should find Josephine another husband quickly so that he could divert her with his behavior instead. But who would want a pragmatic, shrewish, skinny widow?

A man with a strong character to start with. He regarded her warily. Perhaps, one who might even want her for his pleasures, too. It sat ill with him that his brother, Jared, had used her so poorly. From what he could tell, Jared had scarcely spent any time in her bed. She must get lonely with only him and Robert to harass.

He buried the frustration that rose up suddenly over the direction of his thoughts. He would not fall so low as to play matchmaker for Josephine. What she did with her life was none of his business. And his was none of hers. "We dine with Staines and others. I thought to introduce Robert around."

Her face pinched. "About the club—"

Really, this was too much. Was he never to have a moment's peace? "Mrs. Banks," he bit out to silence her. "If you wish to have a lengthy discussion about my life again then I suggest you make an appointment for tomorrow. Right now, we are in the midst of debate over the old mill and you, madam, are interrupting. You've been quite adamant that Robert learn the family business, as it were. Have you changed your mind?"

Josephine blanched at his harsh tone. "No."

"Good. I should not like to have wasted the day on a fool's errand." He waved a hand toward to door. "Until tonight, Mrs. Banks."

Aiden held her gaze as she bobbed a curtsey, and then she turned and fled the room. The door closed loudly.

Beside him, Robert chuckled. "That's telling her." He thumped Aiden's shoulder for good measure as if they were compatriots.

Aiden jumped out of his skin. No one touched him. No one but Terrance and Staines dared.

He stood and tugged down his waistcoat. Putting Josephine in her place had been necessary to stop the flow of her questions, but it had left a bitter taste in his mouth. He would not encourage Robert to laugh at his mother.

Yet, Josephine had been correct. He had barely hidden his good mood during the day. The tryst, a decadent and seductive coupling, had occupied his mind's spare moments all day. He wanted, no needed, to be with Terrance again. He wished he'd not put him off, or that Terrance had not departed so suddenly this morning before they'd made further plans. But at least he knew where to find him.

He stared at the boy until he stopped smiling. "While it is true you must learn to keep others at a necessary distance, if I ever hear you laugh at your mother's discomfort again, I'll box your ears more soundly than if you'd gone ten rounds at Gentleman Jackson's with no respite between."

Robert's mouth fell open and stayed open for quite a while, too. He swallowed suddenly, a mumbled apology tumbling from his lips.

Aiden raked his hands through his hair. Robert sounded as timid as Aiden had been before he'd gained the title. That had to stop. "Do not mumble as if you were nothing larger than a mouse. You will be the Duke of Lewes one day. Learn to act it. One's family may ask anything of you, but not every question must be answered to their satisfaction. Occasionally, your mother has to be reminded she is not in a position to order my life, but our relationship is completely different to yours. She gave you life, boy. Honor her for it."

Robert nodded quickly then bent his head to the papers. Aiden let him work out the calculation alone this time while he paced the room. The mill wasn't worth saving, the damage from the fire too great for the reward from its future labors to counter. He wanted Robert to see that and make his own ruling. The first of many to come, he hoped.

After a while, Robert timidly put forward his assessment, one in line with his own thinking on the matter of rebuilding. His brother's boy was a clever sort. Aiden nodded and had him write the letters for his signature to the estate steward to commence work on a newer site further downstream. Pleased with the afternoon, he sent his nephew away and returned to his bedchamber to change for dinner at the club.

He stood still as his valet, a quiet and unassuming older man, stripped and redressed him without a word. Yet a flare of embarrassment drifted over him as he remembered Terrance rendering the same service to him just this morning. Although he'd enjoyed the sensations of his lover's hands stroking over his body, he should be able to dress himself. As his coat covered his hands and was tugged up into place, Aiden scowled at his reflection. He was next to useless wearing the current fashion of tight sleeves and bordered on the edge of frippery.

Aiden met his valet's gaze. "See to it that all my coats are replaced, Forster. I've rather had enough of these tight fitted sleeves. Have the replacements made looser and perhaps some simpler waistcoats ordered. Never mind if Mr. Weston protests. Pay him double to work fast."

"Yes, Your Grace," Forster replied impassively and departed for the errand. Tomorrow, he'd have new coats to suit his taste. He wouldn't have to wait for Terrance's assistance ever again.

He met his nephew on the stairs and together they crossed London in silence. Aiden's mind fixed on memories of last night. Robert's probably fixed on his ladies of the afternoon prior. However, sex had to wait. Attending the Duke of Staines' dinner at the Hunt Club was more important. He handed off his hat to the major domo and prowled into the Grand Salon.

"Lewes!" Staines shouted, arm raised to wave him over.

As with most nights, Staines had the group of men hanging on his every word, Redding in position some feet behind. Their gazes met, and a slow smile crossed the footman's face before he quickly wiped the expression clean. Damn man. Was it truly that transparent Aiden had been buggered last night and was happy about it?

Staines waved his friends away and turned on him. "Never ever do that to me again."

They both knew he was referring to last night's hurried leave taking in Covent Garden. "Sorry. Couldn't be helped."

Staines smirked at his footman. "Seems to have done the trick for you, however." He turned on Robert. "Mr. Banks, come meet Lord's Clayburn and Chandler. These two fellows will lead you astray quicker than a maid on a stormy night. However, they do give the best parties in all of England. Why at the last one, there was this comely wench who—"

Staines led Robert away and introduced him around. For a moment, Aiden watched the scene, a snippet of the future he intended where he didn't feature, and winced. If all went to plan, Staines would be the one to manage Robert's future. He just didn't know it yet.

He accepted a whiskey from a passing servant and kept track of his heir. Robert glowed under Staines' confidences in a way Aiden found unsettling. He glanced at Redding.

The other man watched too.

Rather than join the other lords, he settled in a chair nearer Redding.

The footman regarded him warily. "I take it you found what you were looking for, Your Grace."

"Yes." Aiden swallowed another mouthful, quite surprised he'd rather converse with Staines' footman than anyone else in the room.

Redding shifted his weight, unobtrusively moving closer to Aiden, affording them greater privacy. "Interesting place Bridgewater's living. That's Byworth's townhouse, by the way, if he didn't explain the situation. Byworth housed his last mistress there."

Blind jealousy rose up to choke Aiden. He ground his teeth over a curse and peered across the room without seeing. If Byworth had touched Terrance, he'd choke him with his own cock.

"Of course, you know Byworth," Redding continued, completely missing Aiden's fury. "He'd do anything for a friend. Even for a lover's friend, it seems."

"Is that so?" Aiden bit out.

"Don't be taking matters the wrong way, Your Grace." Redding shook his head. "Staines had a letter from Byworth today, asking him to keep his eye on Bridgewater, and you, should you meet here in London. Of course, his letter arrived late by a day. Since no trouble came from your renewed acquaintance last night, there's an end to the matter."

Aiden stood and glowered at his friend's footman. "Did

Staines have you follow me?"

"The garden is unsafe, Your Grace. He was right to be concerned." Redding shook his head. "From what I understand, Bridgewater has been hiding under Byworth's roof with Stackpool all along. The pair of them slipped into his household with barely a ripple of interest. Well, except for Stackpool. That one got Byworth's attention from the start."

The haze of red receded. He forced his breathing to slow, for his anger to subside to a reasonable level. But the fury gripping him was still waiting to be unleashed. "So, what was he doing there all this time not to be noticed?" How could anyone with inclinations for bedding other men miss a man of Terrance's appeal? His stomach knotted with jealousy.

Redding pursed his lips. "Oh, he wasn't hiding. He was employed in plain sight as a tutor to the duke's three children." He shook his head. "Not surprising. He was always reading between engagements, so I suppose he discovered other avenues for employment. Yet he took a risk leaving without references, as he did."

Aiden struggled to wrap his mind around the news that Terrance had more than a passing bookish tendency and that Redding admired him for it. When he thought back to last night, he did recall seeing more than a few volumes stacked on a table. Although he wondered what they were about now, his conversation with Redding brought home his apprehension from last night that he knew nothing at all about the man whose pleasures held him in thrall.

But he was terribly keen to learn.

As the bell sounded, Aiden stood to follow the other lords in to dinner, determined to solve the mystery of Terrance Bridgewater. Starting tomorrow, he would leave no stone unturned. He did not care for more surprises.

CHAPTER EIGHT

Terrance took a long draw on his cheroot and blew a near perfect smoke ring into the still night air. This was a pleasure he seldom indulged in, masquerading as an aristocrat out on the town. But the temptation to attend the Henderson annual ball had been too great to ignore.

While society parties might be by invitation only, the larger ones, such as Henderson's, were easy to investigate. No one cared to question a man on his way back from the privy. No one raised a single eyebrow. All Terrance needed to do was jump the wall of the rear garden discreetly, casually smoke a cheroot as if he had all the time in the world, and then slowly join the party as if he were merely returning to the festivities.

He bounded up the terrace steps of the brightly lit great house as if he were eager to see friends. Although many admired him—he'd dressed with particular care so as to blend—no one prevented him from passing into the ballroom.

Just like every other occasion when he'd come here— home to his father's house.

A wave of heat battered his face and the cacophony of music and raised voices assaulted his ears. A smile teased his lips. This was what he loved about London. People. He loved being surrounded by boisterous society. To find out their secrets and vices. To peer beneath the polite layers to see the machinations of ambition beneath.

Although society would never ever know who he was, he kept track of certain individuals that amused him. Lady Russell held court in her scandalous way, all but undressing the gentleman standing across from her with just her eyes. Soon she would seduce the poor fool and add another idiot to her list of many conquests.

But where was the Earl of Danbury? Henderson's

crony was sure to be invited to this sort of event. The crowd shifted, and Terrance was filled with glee. There he was. Short—squat almost—and dancing attendance on a girl half his age yet again. The girl turned and his breath ceased. Not Amelia. Not ever. Terrance eased through the crowd until he had a clearer view and a better chance at eavesdropping.

"Oh, Danbury, you are a tease," Lady Henderson gushed. "Of course, Amelia would dance with you. Come, my dear, show the earl your card. I'm sure you have a waltz free."

Amelia Dunwoody, Henderson's youngest daughter, dithered with her hands behind her back, clearly reluctant to hand the card over. She'd grown up nicely since he'd last laid eyes on her, peeking glimpses at a previous ball before she was allowed out in society. Nice, quiet, and gentle as a lamb—Amelia deserved better than dancing with a lecherous old earl.

Quick as a wink, Terrance snagged the dance card from her fumbling grip as he passed behind her back. He hurried to tuck the card into his breast pocket before he was noticed just as he came face to face with another woman. The stunning blonde quirked an eyebrow, her gaze dipped to his breast pocket where he'd hidden his treasure, and then behind to where a fuss had arisen over 'poor Amelia' and her lost dance card.

A slow smile lifted the corners of the lady's mouth. "Don't let me keep you, sir," the blonde muttered as she passed by his left shoulder.

Quickly, Terrance moved on until he stood some yards away with a pillar between him and Amelia. When he risked a glance, the lady he had encountered had joined Amelia and, judging by their affectionate greeting, seemed a very close acquaintance. He hoped she would take care of Amelia better than her own mother did tonight. Perhaps she could secure her a better dance partner.

He was slipping to have been noticed like that. Perhaps his days as a thief should be left far behind him. Yet it was too much fun to tweak Lord Danbury's nose and deprive him of another opportunity to ogle a young girl.

He looked around him for another source of sport, the Earl of Henderson perhaps, but his attention snagged on the Duke of Lewes and he couldn't look away. Aiden's dark-eyed gaze flittered around those assembled. He appeared uncomfortable here amongst his contemporaries and friends. The Duke of Staines was there, of course, talking expansively to anyone who would listen. Redding too, as always, followed the duke's every word as if his life depended on it.

Even from this distance, he could sense Aiden was only listening to the duke with half an ear. He observed the room's occupants, restless and wary all at once, and then the duke saw him and shock widened his eyes.

Unfortunately, the Duke of Staines' footman noticed him, too. Redding stood taller and took a step forward as if to throw him out. Aiden, finally rousing from his surprise, spoke to him and Redding relaxed.

Then to his delight, Aiden prowled toward him. The tight hand of lust closed upon him as his lover weaved through the crowd, avoiding the dancing couples. They'd never met together in public like this before, and all of Terrance's senses were on alert. What would Aiden do? Would he greet him, scowl at him, or hurry him from the room?

Determined to stand his ground, Terrance leaned against the pillar as if he had every right to be there.

The duke stopped before him. "Mr. Bridgewater."

Terrance smiled with delight as he straightened. "Your Grace. A pleasure to see you again."

A sudden smile flashed over Aiden's face then quickly disappeared. "How are you enjoying your evening?"

"Tolerably good, Your Grace, tolerably good. Lady Henderson has outdone herself on her arrangements. She does like to have everything just so to please her guests."

Aiden turned to face the dancers, shifting subtly until they stood side by side. "Have you had a long association with the Hendersons?"

His pulse sped up at his lover's closer proximity. Mixing in company perhaps wasn't his wisest decision, but he'd wanted to see Aiden again tonight and this was the fastest way to accomplish his goal. "This is my sixth ball, in fact."

A waiter stopped before them with champagne and Terrance snagged a glass to sip before his hands did any incautious wandering toward the duke.

Aiden waved the servant away without taking one. "You look like you belong. I almost didn't believe my eyes when I saw you."

"I told you I was a good actor." He smirked. "I'm imitating you, by the way."

The duke coughed into his fist. "I do not look like that."

"Like what, sinful?" Terrance shifted his weight until his elbow brushed Aiden's. "Damn right you do. Good enough to take down my throat this very night, I think."

A loud pant left Aiden's mouth. Terrance laughed in an effort to suppress the inclination to drag him somewhere private and taste him immediately. Wouldn't Henderson have a fit about that? Although he would like nothing more than to shock the old man, he still had some sense. Protecting Aiden's reputation was paramount. He could suck on his cock later.

Terrance forced his mind away from dark deeds and surveyed the crowd around them. Across the room, the woman he'd collided with earlier was staring at him without blinking. Unnerved by her close scrutiny, he eased nearer to Aiden. "Your Grace, there is a lady watching us quite intently from across the room. Blonde, attractive, olive green ball gown. Do you by any chance know who she is?"

Aiden glanced about and all trace of ease slipped from him. "That is Mrs. Josephine Banks, my sister-in-law."

"Ah." Terrance handed his glass to a passing servant. "A pleasure to see you, Your Grace. Perhaps we will meet another time."

"You're leaving?"

"I fear I must, lest an uncomfortable scene eventuates.

Mrs. Banks seems the questioning sort." Mrs. Banks was also moving in their direction. He had to get out of here. "Will you do me a great favor? A young lady dropped her dance card earlier and since I cannot approach her without a proper introduction, I wondered if you would return it for me. While you're at it, ask her to dance. No decent woman should have Lord Danbury for a partner. Her name is Amelia Dunwoody, Henderson's youngest."

Their fingers brushed as the dance card changed hands.

"I am acquainted with the girl." Aiden's eyebrows rose. "Do you know her well?"

Terrance smiled. "Never had a formal introduction. Be gentle, Your Grace." With a polite nod, he moved away slowly, although his skin cockled with unease and the urge to run. But life had taught him never to show fear before an adversary. He sauntered to a new position around the dance floor and snagged a fresh glass of champagne.

While he sipped, Aiden approached Amelia and, after a brief conversation, drew her toward the dance floor for a waltz. The girl danced very well in Aiden's arms. She smiled prettily and a delightful blush covered the young girl's cheeks, giving her an innocent glow.

Far too innocent for the wicked man society claimed the Duke of Lewes to be.

What Terrance hoped was that the other gentlemen saw and agreed Amelia could do better in their arms. He hoped to incite them to save her from the possibility of an imprudent match. He had nothing at all against Aiden, but Amelia was not for him. Although the duke appeared happy to be dancing with the girl, she would be miserable married to a man of his dark desires.

When the dance ended, Aiden returned Amelia to her gushing mother where other gentlemen waited for their chance. To Terrance's delight, Lord Danbury was firmly pushed from Amelia's circle as younger, jolly gentlemen clamored for her attention. She blushed prettily as her dance card was handed around then she was swept onto the floor again by another imminently more suitable lord.

A smile tugged his lips at the improvement to Amelia's prospects. Tomorrow, if all went to plan, Henderson's drawing room would be full of flowers and potential swains. He hoped she chose wisely from those who came to call. He hoped with all his heart Amelia would be happy.

"That was very well done, sir," a feminine voice muttered at his side.

Terrance turned and discovered Mrs. Banks standing beside him. He groaned aloud. She was definitely trouble. There was no point lying. "So glad you approve, madam."

A low, earthy chuckle passed her lips. "Of course. One must always take care of family, even if one cannot shout it to the world. Amelia is far too young and trusting to associate with the likes of Danbury. My brother-by-marriage has done much for her and himself by standing up with her. But you knew that, didn't you?"

He forced a smile, but alarm bells rang loud in his head. Aiden would not like him to become better acquainted with his sister-in-law. Mrs. Banks had no cause to know him at all. "As you say. Excuse me."

"Wait."

Although he didn't want to, he stopped.

"Lewes is returning." Then she was gone, weaving through the crowd as if the devils chased her.

Terrance turned as Aiden prowled past, a thunderous scowl on his face. Resigned to an awkward conversation, he followed his lover discreetly into the next room, spotted him disappearing through yet another door, and hurried to catch up.

Luckily, that chamber was empty. The door slammed behind his back and he was hauled hard against it. "What the devil did Josephine want with you?"

Terrance pried his neck cloth from Aiden's grip so he could breathe. "She spoke about the good you could do Amelia Dunwoody. That is all."

Aiden's breath passed rough through his mouth. Terrance stared, cock thickening with the hint of danger the duke always exuded when his emotions were aroused. His lover licked his lips and fixed his gaze on his mouth. "Stay away from her."

He curled his arm about Aiden's waist under his coat and rubbed circles over his lower back. "It was never my intention to seek her out. She followed me to the other side of the ballroom. I will not speak to her again."

But his reassurance fell flat. Aiden frowned.

After a long minute, Aiden nodded. "It's for the best."

Terrance tugged hard on Aiden's hips until their cocks brushed. "Want you," he whispered. "But not here."

"Where then?"

His pulse hammered at the need in Aiden's voice. "Come home with me. I'll meet you outside in ten minutes."

"Make it twenty." Aiden whispered against his jaw. "I have to get away from Josephine and Robert first. Could take longer." His lover shifted until their lips brushed lightly.

Terrance flicked his tongue over them in response. "Would you rather meet me at home?"

"No." Aiden eased away. "I'm too damn ready to stand for much of a delay."

"We can fuck standing if you want."

His lover kissed him hard. "Shut that wicked mouth before I shove my cock in it here and now."

He grinned. "As you wish, master."

Aiden rolled his eyes, wrenched the door open and hurried away, leaving him standing in the Earl of Henderson's study. He glanced at the portrait of his mother gracing the wall and shuddered. Terrance crossed the room, plucked her portrait from the wall, and tucked it under his arm.

The first Lady Henderson's portrait belonged with him, not with his bastard of a father.

CHAPTER NINE

Aiden looked up hurriedly as he crashed into someone tall. "Lord Henderson. Forgive me for not watching my step."

"Of course, Your Grace. Think nothing of it." Henderson glanced around them with a fast bob of his head. "See here. Did you perhaps notice a tall gentleman, dark hair, dark suit pass this way? Handsome, I think."

That described half the men in the ballroom, and was a fair description of Terrance, too. A ripple of unease gripped him at Henderson's anxious tone. Aiden sized him up. He'd never heard a whisper that Henderson had less than regular tastes. Still, it wasn't to his benefit to point him in Terrance's direction. The man might have been intimately acquainted with him in the past, and Aiden wasn't about to share his lover again. "No. There is no one else around but me."

"Bollocks." Henderson raked his fingers through his hair. "I could have sworn—"

Aiden frowned. He didn't like hearing the disappointment in Henderson's tone. "If you will excuse me, I should rejoin my party. Excellent evening, Henderson. Your youngest daughter will do well this season."

"Of course." Henderson was all attention at his praise. "Thank you for coming, Your Grace. My daughter will be very pleased by your compliment."

An expectant light brightened Henderson's eyes. Did he think Aiden was interested in little Amelia? That couldn't be farther from the truth. As Terrance had hinted when he'd pressed him to dance with her, Amelia was a gentle girl. Nice enough voice, but nothing in her manner stirred him to reconsider marriage.

The only thing Amelia Dunwoody's wide eyes had reminded him of was Terrance—an unusual occurrence for him to think of a man while dancing with a woman. It was another indication of how affected he was by having Terrance in his life again.

He hurried through the ballroom and pressed the Duke of Staines to escort Josephine and Robert home. His friend nodded as if he expected Aiden's early departure and ignored Redding when he smirked.

As Aiden's coach drew up to the stairs of Henderson House, he spied Terrance waiting in the shadows farther down the driveway, something large clutched in his hands. He waved his carriage away, "I'll not need you, after all. Return to Mercer House." He waited until the carriage departed, then joined Terrance near the shrubbery. "Bridgewater? What have you there?"

"Never mind. This way, Your Grace. I have a hack waiting."

Although curiosity burned through him at Terrance's behavior, he held his tongue where others might overhear any detailed explanation. Why on earth was Terrance holding a painting and where had it come from? An obvious conclusion was that he had stolen it from Henderson's house. After all, paintings of that size in gilded frames hardly lay about on street corners for long.

Even if he had stolen it, why would he?

He settled beside Terrance as he placed the picture on the opposite seat with care. Unfortunately, he'd turned the work around so Aiden had no idea of its nature. Although he'd rather talk the matter over, he set a hand to Terrance's knee.

It had been much too long since last night.

His lover turned, nuzzled his lips before sealing them together in an ardent kiss. Although it had taken some while to grow accustomed to the sensations, Aiden loved kissing now. He couldn't understand how stupid he'd been to deny himself such a simple gift in their previous meetings. Maybe if he had not fought his attraction to Terrance so hard, the last three years might have turned out differently.

He teased his tongue inside Terrance's mouth, running the tip high to swipe the roof of his mouth, along the sharp hard edges of his teeth until his cock ached so badly to be touched he moaned. He almost blurted out a request to be caressed. But he could not trust the driver wouldn't be listening.

Terrance cupped his skull, fingertips skimming over his ear.

Aiden shuddered. "Please."

"Shh," Terrance whispered in return. "We're home."

His stomach lurched. Although his lover hadn't meant the words to be taken so, Aiden was home—with Terrance. He hurried out of the carriage as his mind roiled at the discovery. Wherever this man was, Aiden needed to be. He hadn't thought of the dueling pistol lying within his desk drawer since Terrance had returned to him.

There was no gaping emptiness now that Terrance was back. He no longer wished for an escape from obligations.

Terrance, oblivious to Aiden's revelation, hurried away with the painting clutched to his chest. He opened the door and disappeared inside. Surprised by his quick desertion, Aiden hurried to catch up, moving quietly in case there was a servant lurking. He met with no one and locked the door behind him then peered into the dark house.

The only sounds he heard were coming from Terrance's bedchamber above his head. Aiden tiptoed up the stairs as his lover stirred the fire to life in the dark chamber. He closed the door with a soft click and crossed the room. Watching his lover kneeling by the fire, thigh muscles bunching with tension, brought most of Aiden's lust humming back.

And yet . . . he wanted to know what was going on with that painting. If Terrance had stolen from the Earl of Henderson, then Aiden might be questioned over the matter and potentially be implicated. If that were the case, he'd need to come up with a plausible suggestion that would turn attention away from him, and from Terrance.

Aiden craned his neck and spotted the painting, face turned toward the wall, on the far side of the bed. As he took a step toward it, Terrance stood, crossed the room, and crushed him to his chest.

A rough gasp passed his lover's lips as his hands flowed over Aiden's body, all too clearly revealing how much he was wanted tonight.

The feeling was entirely mutual, but . . . the painting? "Terrance, wait."

"Done with waiting." He pushed Aiden's ridiculously tight fitting coat from his shoulders and opened his waistcoat, then set about removing his cravat. "Turn around so I can strip you. I've got a surprise."

"Shh," Aiden hissed. "For God's sake, keep your voice down." What the hell was wrong with him to take no care that they were undiscovered?

Terrance chucked. "No need tonight. We have the house to ourselves. I sent the servants away with a handful of coins each. They were very keen to go." He drew a line down Aiden's cheek. "Be as loud as you want. There's no one to overhear our enjoyment."

"Oh!"

"Oh, indeed." Terrance spun Aiden around, his hands stroking his chest hard and then he pinched his nipple through his shirt.

Aiden moaned as his desire roared back to life. His cock pushed at the placket of his trousers as his lover teased him without mercy, pulling and rolling his nipples without ease. He arched his neck as Terrance nipped the column of his throat. He'd never get enough of this. Every time they met he wanted more. It had always been that way, even when Terrance claimed he'd been merely acting the tyrant.

Unwilling to be the sole recipient of attention, he slipped a hand behind his back and captured Terrance's cock where it stood out within his trousers. The hard length burned his palm, even through gentleman's clothing. He shuddered at how much he wanted to be buggered tonight. To be possessed by the man whose every move held him in thrall.

Terrance moaned and nipped Aiden's ear, then feathered his tongue along the rim. A shudder raced through him as his lover tore his shirt clear down the middle. Terrance pulled him nearer until Aiden's hand could barely move over his lover's cock. He gave up, relishing the anticipation of being possessed by such fierce need.

His waistcoat and ruined shirt were whisked away. "Raise your arm," Terrance whispered between nips to Aiden's shoulder.

He complied, raising both hands upward, holding them a few feet apart. His lover captured one and looped a rope tied to the bedpost around his wrist, then snagged the other, and tied it to the first. He stood, cock aching for release, both hands bound above his head to the same carved pole. The position was one he had been in before. He could turn if he chose to, or if Terrance chose to let him.

He twisted to see what movement he was allowed.

He met Terrance's gaze as his lover moved closer. They kissed, tongues tangling fast and desperate, hips rutting against one another to heighten the need.

It wasn't anywhere near close enough. Aiden pulled on the ropes binding him, eager to close the miniscule gap as his lover licked and kissed down his chest, hands skimming his flesh and setting little fires of lust in their wake. Terrance fell to his knees, and opened his mouth over Aiden's straining cock, fabric and all.

He pulled harder on the rope, and harder again, as his trousers were opened and his cock encountered warmth.

He looked down as Terrance ran his tongue over the head, licking at the moisture beaded on the tip with one long, soft lick. He bucked his hips, pushing his cock closer to that wonderful mouth. It had been a long time since Terrance had tried this when Aiden had so much movement.

The coils of rope round his wrists chafed the way previous leather restraints had not. He forced himself to calm, even as his lover swallowed his cock deeper into his mouth.

The wet heat and suction forced him to close his eyes and he groaned loudly. My God, Terrance could take a man and make him forget he was a gentleman. He shifted his hips, rocking his cock in and out past those willing lips, wishing he might hold his lover against him at the same time.

That had not been his wish before. He'd been uncomfortable with Terrance's face buried in his groin or arse.

As if sensing the turn of his thoughts, Terrance parted his arse cheeks and brushed the tip of a finger over Aiden's hole.

"Fuck, don't do that yet," Aiden growled, staring across the room rather than at his lover as his balls drew up. He was so close to coming that he couldn't stand the added stimulation right now. He'd spend like a green lad if that happened.

Terrance released his cock and Aiden let out a relieved breath. The pace was too quick tonight, the need too raw and desperate. He wanted all night in his lover's bed, not a few frantic minutes, even if they were exactly what he had loved best in the past. But then Terrance kissed his bollocks.

In an attempt to hold off his pleasure, he looked up at the ropes binding him. A simple slip knot. He could be free in an instant if he chose.

Terrance forced one of Aiden's legs up until it rested on the bed. The spread, helpless position caused a deep rumbling groan from his lover's lips. He stood and ripped off his trousers, revealing the thick arch of cock Aiden loved.

But he only got the briefest glimpse. Terrance fell to his knees again, then buried his face far beneath Aiden's bollocks and licked the smooth skin behind. The sensation forced Aiden up onto the toes of one foot and he twisted helplessly on the rope. Hell, he was so aroused he'd spend over his lover's smooth muscled back.

The idea, the image of his seed sliding over any part of Terrance's skin, excited him unbearably. Too much. Far too much.

He tugged the rope until his hands were free and he stumbled away from his lover.

Terrance growled. "Aiden?"

He held out one hand, silently begging his aching cock to subside and Terrance to keep a distance. He set his hands to his knees as his breath churned in and out roughly. When he thought he had better control, he looked up.

A mistake.

Terrance stood waiting, hand stroking his cock slowly, pale seed weeping from the tip in a long string.

Aiden rushed him and threw him on the bed, pinning him in place with his body.

CHAPTER TEN

Terrance gasped as his lover covered him and kissed him with animal like ferocity. He'd never expected Aiden to free himself, although he'd certainly tied the rope with that possibility in mind. He'd expected the duke to want to stay bound though, and his early escape and subsequent behavior set hope soaring through his heart.

It was nice to be wanted so fiercely. It made the possessive thoughts swirling through his mind easier to bear.

He rubbed his hips against the silky softness of his lover's cock and set a new course for the night. No games. No limitations. No regrets.

He flipped his lover to his back and pushed up from the bed.

"Don't go," Aiden begged.

Terrance ruffled his hair gently and grinned. "When I come back, I'm going to possess you, my lord duke. I'm going to make you beg and moan and if I'm very, very lucky, you'll scream."

"Is that a threat?" Aiden licked his lips, an inviting sight that tempted him to lean forward and kiss him soundly.

But for the next step in their bedroom adventures, they both had to be calmer. "No. It is my promise to you." Terrance swung off the bed to collect the bottle of oil, then climbed back up beside Aiden. He smoothed the strands of his lover's hair again and then straddled his chest.

Aiden wriggled beneath him. "What are you going to do with that oil?"

He smiled. "Nothing yet." He slid the bottle beneath a pillow for later, and then curled a hand around Aiden's skull. With his other hand, he presented the head of his cock to his lover. "Open your mouth."

Although it seemed Aiden might protest, he shifted until his breath brushed over the head of Terrance's cock. His lover made a tentative sweep to taste the abundant seed leaking from the tip and a moan escaped his control.

Damn he wanted this man forever.

The thought brought his raging lust back under control.

Impossibilities were all he could dream. He and Aiden had no future in London.

He gently guided Aiden's lips closer to his cock again and gasped as he opened his mouth willingly to swallow the head. The hot flicks of his tongue reduced Terrance to near mindlessness, but he fought the sensations, urging Aiden to take more. To take him as deep into him as he could bear.

His lover's eager participation and acceptance of their mutual lust made his heart ache. They were so good together now that neither was pretending not to want the other. So good, in fact, that he might spill in his mouth.

He did not want that tonight.

He had to stay in control as long as he could. But watching Aiden's cheeks hollow and fill as he learned how to suck him wasn't such a good idea. The occasional scrape of teeth excited him too much.

Reluctantly, he removed his cock from Aiden's mouth, letting his cock slide slowly over full, swollen lips. A whimper escaped his lover as he moved to lie down on his side. He reached for the oil and opened it. Aiden started to turn.

"No. Don't go," he commanded. "Stay as you are, but pull your knees toward your chest."

Quickly, Terrance spread the oil over his full cock, then between Aiden's spread cheeks. His lover hissed and moaned, clearly enjoying the sensations. Carefully, he inserted two fingers into Aiden's arse, knowing the swift tight stretch would excite Aiden as much as it did him.

When Aiden was prepared and ready, Terrance covered him with his body, easing between his bent legs until his cock was nestled where it ached to be. Aiden's eyes widened as Terrance arranged him as he wished—one leg over his shoulder, the other thigh in his grip.

Carefully he pressed in, watching Aiden's face for the first time ever. His lover winced as he put greater pressure on the tight band of muscles of his arse. Terrance kept his pressure steady, even, and after Aiden let out a long breath, he slowly sank deep. Not deep enough, however. He pulled back a bit then slowly worked his length deeper as Aiden moaned and gasped.

His lover shut his dark eyes briefly as he buried to the hilt, when he opened them again they glowed brightly with emotion. Slowly, Terrance pistoned his cock in and out of his lover's arse—barely keeping his rising need in check.

When Aiden's leg muscles relaxed to softness, Terrance dragged him closer until his bollocks rested against flesh. The touch loosened his control, and he fucked Aiden harder than before. The slap of his nuts against flesh brought a moan tumbling out, answered by Aiden in equal measure.

"Beat your cock in time with me, lover," Terrance demanded.

Aiden swiftly captured himself, long fingers wrapping around the hard length and kept time with Terrance's pressure on his arse.

He swore. "Fuck me, but you are a damn sinful man, Aiden Banks. I'm going to make your arse burn so you never forget me." With that, he turned his hip, widening Aiden's legs and setting a furious pace.

Beneath him, Aiden huffed and grunted, his hand shuttling over his smooth cock. Terrance released one leg, swiped his fingers over the head until they were wet. He met Aiden's gaze as he raised his hand to his mouth then sucked the moisture from his digits. The duke gasped, and swore, and screamed. Thick spurts of pale seed shot up his chest and the sight proved too much for Terrance to ignore.

He fucked Aiden without mercy as his seed boiled from his cock, then shouted Aiden's name as he came violently. He fell over Aiden, sliding on slick skin and pale seed. He fought for breath and control of his emotions, but feared he was lost. He did not want to want Aiden like this. He had no right to wish for more.

Yet his heart was breaking over leaving him tomorrow.

Against all odds, Aiden was the greatest threat to his contentment. His lover made him want forever.

Fearing he was about to weep in an unmanly fashion, Terrance crawled off Aiden and collapsed on his back.

For a long time neither spoke, only gasped for breath.

But then Aiden rolled onto his side to look at him. "Are you all right?"

Terrance turned his head, falling into the dark eyes of the man he suspected he might have stupidly fallen in love with. "Are you?"

A grin tugged up the corners of Aiden's mouth. "Christ, I felt you at the back of my throat. I want that again."

He didn't return the smile. A deep sadness gripped him. He had to tell Aiden he was leaving England before his lover started making plans for tomorrow, or next week, or far longer. "Perhaps you'll not be needing me when I get back."

Aiden frowned. "Get back? Are you going somewhere soon?"

He tucked one arm behind his head and took a deep breath. "I'm leaving England tomorrow. Or is it today?"

"No." Aiden sat up swiftly.

Terrance sat up, dangling his legs over the side of the bed. "I have no future in England. I want to travel, to see the world I've only read about in books and the newssheets. Thanks to my last position, I have the funds to do it. Tomorrow, I travel south to find passage on the first ship that takes my fancy. Wish me well, Aiden. I'm off on my first adventure."

Aiden made no sound behind him.

Fearing the duke was about to explode with anger, Terrance turned his head but met liquid brown eyes.

"You cannot leave me again. Not ever." Aiden's chest heaved as though he struggled to contain his emotions.

The tight choke of regret gagged any response

Terrance wanted to utter. Leaving London, and England, was the correct thing to do. He may have been born into Aiden's world but he no longer belonged there. He could not drag Aiden into his life more than this. He stood on shaky legs and for something to do with his hands, he removed the long coil of rope from the bedpost.

Aiden hissed. "You are not leaving without me. I'm coming with you."

Terrance lifted his head to stare at the duke. "Don't be ridiculous. Your place is here."

"My place is with you." He threw himself off the bed and crushed Terrance to him. "I'll not stand to be parted from you again. I won't allow it."

Although his words were probably meant from the heart, what Aiden suggested was impossible. A duke did not up and follow his gentleman lover to the far side of the world on a whim. Come tomorrow, he'd change his mind about it all and eventually laugh at his ridiculous response.

Terrance curled his arms about Aiden and squeezed. He should have known his lover would react so strongly to the news. He reacted strongly to everything else. Perhaps he shouldn't have told him, just disappeared from his life again like last time. But Aiden had become a different man since then. He allowed himself to be fragile and had placed his trust in Terrance. He rocked his lover in his arms until he pulled away.

Aiden crossed the room and snatched up the painting. When he turned it around, an astonished frown creased his brow. "But this is Lady Henderson. The former Lady Henderson. Why would you take this?"

Terrance took the portrait from his hands and placed it face out on an armchair. His mother's smiling face peeked back at him, exactly as he remembered her from long ago. He could almost imagine the lingering hint of roses in the room now that her portrait was with him. He missed her. He loved her. He'd never lose her again.

He turned to face Aiden, waving a hand toward the portrait with regret. "My mother."

Aiden's mouth opened in astonishment. Then he

snapped it shut without a word.

While he was silent, Terrance righted the room, tossing strewn clothing on another chair in preparation for the morning. When he was done, he climbed into bed and let his gaze fall on his mother once more.

Aiden moved to stand between him and the painting. "Lady Henderson's only son died with her."

"So I've heard many a time." Terrance settled on his side as long-fought memories rose and fell restlessly. He blotted them out by thinking of Aiden's smooth cock sliding over his tongue. It was better to think of the present instead of the disappointments of the past.

He closed his eyes as the bed dipped. Aiden climbed in behind him. When his lover snuggled up against his back and hugged him tightly to his chest, Terrance weakened and turned over. He embraced his lover hard as tears flowed from his eyes.

Aiden accepted his lapse of control without a word, smoothing his hands over Terrance's shaking back, holding his head firmly to his shoulder. When he was empty and numb once more, he grabbed a corner of the sheet to blot his weeping eyes. He couldn't look at his lover now, not after that outpouring of troubling emotion. He kept his head tucked away and settled in for sleep.

The last thing he remembered before oblivion claimed him was Aiden's repeated whisper, "I'm definitely coming with you."

CHAPTER ELEVEN

A week ago Aiden would not have given another man's discomfort a moment's thought, but Terrance's refusal to look him in the eye, or speak more than one word at a time had him scrambling for the correct words to utter. Last night's startling revelation of his lover's connections, his astoundingly lofty origins, had silenced both of them. He didn't know what to think. He sat down in the cold kitchen and reached for a piece of cheese.

Terrance shifted restlessly in his seat. "It's not what you're used to, I'm sure."

Aiden quickly swallowed the food in his mouth without tasting it. "Are you saying I'm spoiled?"

A sad smile twisted Terrance's lips. "You're used to the best. To me, this is a feast. I should warn you that I don't expect to eat much better on my adventure. You should stay where you belong."

"My adventure, too." Yet a tumbling disquiet stirred Aiden. He sat forward. "Do you want to tell me what happened to Viscount Hathaway? If memory serves, he was very young at the time of his reputed death."

Terrance stood abruptly and walked to the open rear door. He stood looking out, tense, muscles clenching and unclenching alarmingly. He wrapped his arms tight about his chest. "His mother pushed him from the carriage as the swollen river swept them downstream. She didn't follow him out as she promised she would."

"That was a brave thing to do." Aiden could imagine such a scene. "She must have loved you very much."

"The only one who did." Terrance set his head to the doorframe. "It would have been better to have drowned together," he whispered.

"Don't say that," Aiden snapped.

"Why not?" Terrance shouted. "Surely death would have been preferable to what happened to me after and being forgotten entirely."

The agony behind his words brought moisture to Aiden's eyes. He crossed the room and leaned against Terrance's back, not holding him but offering his support should it be needed. "What happened to you?"

"Something no child should ever be a witness to. Sickness, madness." His voice trailed off on the last words and a shudder rocked him. "I wanted to die so many times. But I was never alone. I was taken by a collector. There were more children, all weeping and scared like me. The number rose and fell every day. I don't know to this day where they came from or where they went."

A lump formed in Aiden's throat. He curved his arm slowly around Terrance's waist. "Yet you survived."

"I was fortunate. A servant left the door unlatched and a few of us slipped out. We stayed together for a while, stealing what we needed without any thought but survival. Wild savages every last one of us. One day I came across a wagon stopped by the side of the road, the driver taking a piss behind a tree. Since it was heading in the direction I wanted to go, I hid myself and, after a while, ended up in London. I was eight by then."

Aiden curled his other arm about Terrance and set his chin to his shoulder. "Why did you not tell someone who you were? Had you forgotten?"

Terrance spun out of his arms. "Did you think I did not try? I shouted to everyone who had ears that I was Viscount Hathaway, a rich man's son, Lord Henderson's son. Not one blasted person in his London townhouse believed me. I told them my father would whip them for the wrong they did me. Instead of heeding my words they dragged me away and. . ." He rushed outside.

Aiden followed as Terrance vomited his breakfast over the garden beds. He set a hand to his lover's broad back as his shoulders heaved. He could only guess at what might have happened to Terrance to make him react so strongly. He must have felt so terribly betrayed. It seemed a miracle he'd survived.

Terrance pulled away, a bitter laugh bursting through his lips. "I thought my father would search for me. I thought he would move heaven and earth to bring me home. Instead, I discovered he married within six months and produced three daughters in quick succession. He never gave me or my mother a second thought. I visited the house the first time to confront him, but then I found her painting hanging in the house and simply stared at it. I couldn't take the painting with me until now."

Aiden found it hard to believe Henderson had forgotten his son but he could understand the quick second marriage. Such a scenario happened all too often after a sudden death of an heir. Lord Aiden ached to hold his lover again, yet they were outside in broad daylight. Anyone might see. He tugged on Terrance's arm. "Come back inside and sit down."

Terrance nodded and shuffled toward the house, his movements limp, drained of vigor, and utterly terrifying. Aiden pushed him to the bench and passed his glass of wine over. Terrance drained it and then another.

Aiden sat beside him. "Thank you for sharing what was obviously a harrowing experience. You don't have to say more if it upsets you this much. But I will listen any time you want to speak of it, again."

Terrance regarded him in silence. Eyes dull, agile lips stiff. The bright spark of mischief was absent from his eyes.

Aiden thought he might know how to get it back. He ran his hand lightly over Terrance's skull and sifted his fingers through the long strands. "Now. About this trip. Where are you taking me?"

"You don't have to pretend you're coming, Your Grace. It's enough that you thought you wanted to last night."

"Of course I'm coming. Can't let you have all that fun alone. If you could extend your departure date by a few days, though, I'd appreciate it. Josephine will likely argue non-stop when she learns."

"The Duke of Lewes has responsibilities," Terrance argued.

"Yes, he does. He needs to keep Viscount Hathaway from getting lost. Not that we'll make use of our titles while we're abroad. I've traveled a bit myself and they just get in the way." He curled an arm about Terrance's shoulders. "I cannot wait to travel the world with you."

"God damn it," Terrance hissed, pressing his fingers to his eyes.

"I am determined, Terry." Aiden chuckled. "You're not escaping me now."

"Terry?"

He grinned. "Thought I'd try it out. There is so much about you I want to uncover. Do you hate the name?"

"Only my mother called me that."

"May I, too?"

Terry nodded slowly.

Aiden shook him. "Good, tell me where we are off to first?"

Although he would like nothing more than to pry every secret from him here and now, he judged he'd pushed enough for one day. While Terry listed the places he thought would be most interesting, Aiden ran a hand up and down his leg, soothing his lover as best he could. The nightmare that had been his childhood was still too raw and brutal, even after so many years had passed. He didn't understand how he could bear the pain but he had always been strong. He'd had to be. He may not be able to erase the wrongs done to him, but he would offer his support the only way he knew how.

Touch. Terry thrived on sensations. Aiden drew Terry into his arms and held him tightly against his chest. He could give his lover the gift of his affections with the hope he'd never feel so abandoned again.

After a long time of stillness, he glanced out the door at the bright new day dawning upon them. "I should go to make my preparations, but I'll return tonight to let you know when I can be ready to depart."

"Of course," Terry's reluctant response made Aiden smile.

He kissed him hard. "Until tonight."

In truth, Aiden didn't want to leave. But he had to pack and face Josephine and Robert, eventually. Then he would always be with Terry. The short distance passed in a blur of excitement and when the door of Mercer House shut soundly behind him, he found Josephine, pale and trembling, waiting on the staircase.

His eagerness died. "What on earth are you doing sitting there?"

She stood suddenly, descended the stairs and flew at him. But instead of the lecture he expected for leaving her last night without so much as a goodbye, she embraced him. "Thank God you're home."

He pulled her arms from about his neck. "Josephine, we need to talk."

"We certainly do. I could have killed someone."

Aiden frowned. "What's that you say?"

"I could have shot someone." She gestured behind her. "The pistol was primed."

Aiden hurried for his study. A lingering scent of gun smoke permeated the room, a bookcase shelf splintered from a shot. His pistol, spent now, lay on his desk in silent accusation. He turned about as Josephine joined him. "What the devil were you doing in my desk drawer?"

"What were you doing with a loaded pistol?" She countered, hands settling on her hips. "You are always playing with something in that drawer. Every time I come in here you shut it."

"Never mind why. Do you have no respect for my privacy? Or anyone's for that matter?"

"Of course I respect your privacy. If I didn't I'd have asked different questions about your life. Why you've suddenly become happy, for instance. After last night's ball, I have guessed at the reason."

His throat tightened. Surely she couldn't know about his preference for other men—especially for Terry. He met her gaze. "What about last night?"

He really didn't want her to answer, though.

Josephine approached his desk and handed him the daily news sheet. "Henderson's study was robbed last night during the ball."

He took the paper, swallowing hard as he read quickly over the article. *No witnesses to the theft. Painting stolen. Much loved.* He dropped the paper as if it burned him. "Very distressing."

"I had a note from Amelia Dunwoody just this morning," Josephine continued. "She says her father is on the rampage, her mother in tears. It seems the painting in question, a portrait of the late Lady Henderson, is a source of great unrest between the earl and his countess."

"That is surprising."

"What's more surprising is that your acquaintance bore a startling resemblance to young Amelia. There is something about their eyes that soothes the soul." She gripped his arms. "An unacknowledged illegitimate son will gain no sympathy with such acts of thievery. You must have him return the painting immediately."

"Would you say the same if he was a legitimate heir?" Aiden cursed his tongue. He should not have asked her that.

Josephine's fingers trembled over her lips. "Legitimate, you say?"

Reluctantly, he nodded.

"Oh. Well now, that changes everything. He should come forward."

"He will not."

"But why?" Her brow scrunched. "If he is who I imagine he could be, he will be an earl eventually. Sooner if Lord Henderson has an apoplexy over the missing painting. "

He couldn't tell her the circumstances of Terry's past. Even he didn't understand the vast hurt the man carried. "Josephine, you cannot meddle in this. He will not come forward. He's leaving England." He took a deep breath. "And so am I. I'm going with him."

Josephine nodded. "A good plan. A bit of time, a bit of polish, and tutoring in the social graces and he will be better prepared for the storm that is sure to erupt over his return."

Aiden gaped. "What the devil are you blathering about woman? We are not coming back."

"You are not leaving us with your responsibilities indefinitely, Aiden Banks." She drew in a deep breath and let it out slowly. "I know just how it should happen.

You will discover the dashing Viscount Hathaway in your travels and return triumphantly to London together. How else can you explain your close acquaintance with the man?"

He opened his mouth and shut it again. What Josephine proposed was too ludicrous for words. Yet a small part of his mind registered her brilliance. If Terry wanted to return one day, traveling could be a valid reason for him not to be known in England. Even if the gentlemen he'd entertained at the Hunt Club recognized him, they'd never breathe a word. The members of the Hunt Club and even staff were sworn to secrecy.

Could Terry take his rightful place in society? Would he want to one day?

The decision wasn't his to make. But, if that was what Terry wanted, they could return together as close friends without a great many questions asked about how they met. He settled into a chair, thinking about a life here with Terry in the public eye. Could they disguise their attachment successfully?

He lifted his head. Josephine was grinning. "It will work. When you decide to return, you must write me with the astonishing news of your discovery of Henderson's heir and I will gently inform his lordship that his son has been found alive and well. Since Henderson has another family now, you can offer to house the viscount here and no one will think it the least bit odd."

"No one will think it the least bit odd?" he repeated.

Josephine sank to her knees at his feet and took his hand. "This is better than what that pistol was meant for, isn't it, Aiden?" she whispered.

He twisted his hands to loosen her grip.

She clung. "I saw you that morning with him on the street outside and last night together at the ball. He makes you happy and that is all I will ever care about. I may not like your plan to travel, but Robert and I will bumble along until your return. When you come back to us, I will be easy again." She rose up and kissed his cheek. "Be very careful and don't stay away too long."

CHAPTER TWELVE

Terrance roused himself from his slump and looked about him. The day had flown while he'd sat lost in memories of the past and plans for the future. He could not believe that Aiden would come with him. Yet part of him hoped for his company. A very great part.

He glanced about the cold kitchen. Finnegan and his wife would return that afternoon and he had better make himself scarce, lest they think him snooping in their domain. He crossed to the rear door and was about to latch it when a shadow moved in the rear yard. He stilled as a squat shape shifted in the rear shed's shadow. Then the shadow broke in half.

Two small children crept closer to the house. Two very grubby children, one he recognized as the boy from his first day in London, the other he didn't. The scamp that had benefited from his pilferage of a wallet had indeed followed him home in search of more and brought a friend with him. Terrance's heart ached at the sight of them. Torn clothes, gaunt cheeks and a bruise across the largest one's jaw.

He curled his hand into a fist, remembering all too well the pain and confusion he'd felt the first time he'd been beaten. Forcing his hand to unclench, Terrance opened the door slowly so they didn't startle. They froze when he was fully visible to them, prepared for flight at any moment. He exited the house.

The boy looked to be about nine. The other was a snotty nosed girl a few years younger. The two children clustered together. "Don't come any closer," the boy warned.

His polished accents surprised Terrance. "Stay back?" he asked softly. "But you are in my garden. You followed me here, remember."

They would want food, and a safe place to stay at

night. He could offer them the first. The other he couldn't manage beyond tomorrow. A pity. They looked like they could use a friend. He crouched down on his haunches so he wasn't quite so tall and intimidating to them. "What are your names?"

"Gerard Prichard and this is my sister, Maggie."

The little one peeked around her brother, large uncertain eyes stirring up memories of other frightened children, children gone and forgotten by all but him. "Pleased to meet you, Master Gerard and Miss Maggie."

The pair shifted restlessly. Their clothes—once fine now decidedly shabby—at odds with his first impression of thieves. They were discarded children, just as he had once been.

"Are you hungry?"

Their eyes widened, teeth biting into the soft flesh of their lips to control their response. *Poor lambs.* Only the hope of feeding their aching bellies had brought them this close to his door.

Terrance stood. "There's food in the kitchen."

He pivoted and returned to the kitchen without seeing whether they followed. He kept the door wide while he clattered around the cupboards, seeking enough food to satisfy them both. As he set out his findings on the table, the little girl scampered onto a bench, clenched her hands in her lap, and daintily crossed her ankles. Her brother warily took a spot closest to the door.

"Eat what you like. I'll just fetch more firewood and get a nice blaze going to warm you."

While Terrance went about relighting the fire and fetched water and a washbasin, he cursed himself for getting involved. He was leaving England as soon as Aiden was ready. It was cruel to give them hope for a permanent benefactor. Yet, as he paused to observe them, his foolish heart clattered. They were too young to be all alone. Children of their age were the most vulnerable to cruel use by adults they hoped would aid them.

He sat at the head of the table, sipping on a glass of wine while they ate. "Where do you hail from Gerard?"

The boy's gaze darted about the room. "London."

When he didn't elaborate, Terrance leaned back in the chair. "London is a big place. It's easy to get lost in it. I was lost once. I was very scared at first."

"We're not lost," Maggie quipped decisively. "We ran away."

"Is that so?" He glanced at the boy, but he wouldn't meet his gaze. "Will you go home one day?"

"No." Gerard's single word rang with finality and a generous flare of anger.

Were Maggie's words a tall tale to hide something else?

The pair of them did not appear as other homeless children did. They hadn't tried to steal anything so far and that in itself surprised him. He'd expected to be firm with them about not touching the contents of the room around them. Gerard hadn't even admired the silver salt shaker at his elbow. Maggie seemed completely comfortable in the house, too, licking grease from her fingertips daintily. She sniffed. Her runny nose bothered him.

He withdrew his handkerchief. "Come here, Maggie. Let me look after your nose?"

She glanced at his hand holding the handkerchief and then her brother. When Gerard nodded, she moved to stand before him. He wiped her nose gently and had her blow her nose as he would have done with Lord Byworth's daughter. A lock of her hair slipped forward over her eyes and he stumbled back. It crawled with lice. "Bugger me," Terrance swore.

The children raced for the door.

"Wait," he called. They looked at him, fear in their eyes. He sat down again. "My apologies, but your sister has lice in her hair. They took me by surprise, that is all. I didn't mean to sound cross."

The boy relaxed. "We both do."

Maggie burst into tears. "They won't go away. Make them go away. I hate them!" Then she sobbed so pitifully Terrance's heart quaked. He couldn't abandon them to the dangers found beyond his door. He could help them, protect them as he wasn't, very easily.

He handed her his handkerchief again. "Nothing that cannot be fixed and soon. Come back to the fire and rest."

Reluctantly, Maggie perched on Cook's chair.

But Terrance had no idea how to solve the problem of their hair quickly. It was an age since he'd suffered the affliction. He looked about the chamber for a comb.

"What's all this sobbing about?"

Terrance looked up as Finnegan and his wife barged into the room.

"Ah," Terrance began, glancing at the children quickly. "They followed me home and will be staying as long as they like."

Finnegan gave him a long measured look. "You do bring all types with you. Children? Whatever will be coming next?"

He winced. "There is a slight dilemma for the pair. They have some small company nested in their hair. Miss Maggie is most particularly distressed by them, hence the tears. Master Gerard less so, but the situation needs immediate attention."

Finnegan's wife gave the girl a warm smile. "Are you hungry, lass?"

"No thank you," Maggie hiccupped.

"Then would you like to wash up now that you've eaten? There's a hip bath somewhere in the attic."

Maggie's eyes grew to saucers, "A real bath?" She nodded, her eyes filling with tears.

Only a well-bred child would prefer a soaking to a measly wash.

Terrance held Gerard's gaze. "Finnegan, would you attend to Master Gerard's comfort while I'm out? There are a few things the children need, as you can see."

The boy swallowed and looked at the floor as he nodded. Poor lad, he'd have done the best he could for his sister. But he certainly shouldn't manage the burden alone.

Finnegan slapped him on the shoulder. "Are you going to keep them, sir?"

The children stared, both sets of eyes brimming with

hope.

He nodded. "I believe I will. I'll be back as soon as I can."

Finding what the children needed from the unfamiliar businesses on Bond Street proved a bigger hurdle than Terrance had first anticipated. He was very late returning to Mill Street and hoped the servants hadn't resigned on the spot from dealing with lice and whatever muck coated the poor children. He'd never purchased for children before and had used another customer's children to guess at the sizes he needed. Hopefully, they would fit well enough until he could have proper garments made. Given what they'd suffered through, Gerard and Maggie should be pleased. He let himself in with his key and hurried for the kitchen.

A male throat cleared to his right. "Would you mind telling me why there are children asleep in your sitting room, Mr. Bridgewater?"

Terrance spun, jostling his burdens to see Aiden leaning against a doorway. "You're early."

"I'm all but ready to depart on our adventure." His lips turned down. "However, it seems there has been a change in your situation. You have offspring, I'm told."

"They are not mine," he said quickly.

The duke's brow rose.

"They followed me home."

His lips quirked. "We have something in common it seems."

Terrance hadn't thought how Aiden would take the news of his plan to assume responsibility for the children until this moment. But it was far too late to change his course now. He rushed ahead.

"Goodness," Finnegan chuckled, "did you get enough for the wee things?"

Terrance wiped the sweat from his brow with one finger. "Possibly. I'm not sure of the fit, however."

Finnegan's wife laid out his purchases. "They'll fit with

a few nips and tucks on Miss Maggie's garments. I will work on them tonight. The children got tired of waiting for your return and fell asleep where they sat. Dinner will be served in an hour. I take it the gentleman will be dining with you this evening?"

"He will," Aiden said from the door.

"Very good, my lord." Cook bobbed. "I'll dress the children in time for their supper. Their bedchamber will be closer to ours, if you don't mind, sir. I don't want to be traipsing the house and disturbing your rest this evening." A mischievous sparkle lit her eyes. "You're very kind."

As he turned, Finnegan muttered under her breath. "Can't have the little ones getting too early an education of the ways of the world, now can we?"

Damnation. Finnegan and his wife had guessed. Anxiety turned his mouth to ashes. They'd not been careful enough.

He snagged Aiden's arm and drew him toward the small library. When the door closed behind his back, he leaned upon it. "Slight change of plan."

"Such as."

"The children are coming with me."

Aiden's eyes widened in surprise. "I thought you'd say you were staying here with them. Not dragging them off into the unknown. Whose children are they anyway?"

"I don't know." He frowned. "But I know what it's like to be in their situation. I cannot turn away from them when I can save them. Do you know what will happen to them on the street without someone stronger to protect them."

"I can guess you fear it will be what happened to you." Aiden came close. "You are a remarkably kind man. If you are sure."

"As sure as I am about you," he blurted, heart filling with relief. He'd never known Aiden to care for children so his easy acceptance meant a lot. Terrance cupped his hands around his lover's jaw. "Thank you."

He brushed his lips lightly across Aiden's.

The duke pulled away, a frown appearing. "Did you

read in the paper today that there was a theft at Lord Henderson's ball last night?"

Terrance shrugged. "What is Henderson to me? I'm hardly the sort to be invited to his ball. I'm sure he will get over his disappointment in due time."

Aiden growled softly. "My sister-in-law is quite friendly with Amelia Dunwoody and had a note from. Seems the Henderson's are in an uproar over the disappearance. Lord Henderson wants that painting back. It must be dear to him."

He folded his arms across his chest. "I'm sure it's not."

Aiden approached, set his hands to Terrance's hips and kneaded. "Do you want to regain your proper position? My sister-in-law thinks you should."

Terrance frowned. "You told Mrs. Banks about me?"

The duke scoffed. "The only secret that can be kept from that woman is one she'd rather forget. By the way, your eyes are remarkably similar to Amelia's. I was reminded of you the whole time we danced. Mrs. Banks noticed too."

"Amelia is a sweet girl."

Aiden shook him. "Who does not know she has a half-brother looking out for her interests. She should."

He shrugged, but his stomach roiled with thoughts of his half-sister. She might like him as a fake footman, but a brother? That would be anyone's guess. "My reappearance would cause her distress."

"What if her errant brother returned home from a trip abroad with much fanfare and anticipation? Josephine has a touch of the dramatic at times. She thinks I should discover you on my trip and announce it to Henderson and all of society. I'm afraid Josephine is looking forward to her part in it all. But, of course, it is entirely up to you. I will be happy wherever you are, you know that?"

Terrance curled a hand about Aiden's skull and drew him forward for a kiss. "We're still leaving. Mrs. Banks will have to live with disappointment."

Aiden smiled as if he really didn't mind Terrance turning his back on his past and, when they kissed again contentment trickled through him. He could not wait 'till their days kept them together. In fact, the idea of joining with him right now seemed a very good idea. He dropped a hand around Aiden's arse and kneaded the firm globe until his lover groaned. Perhaps a quick release before dinner was in order. He sank to his knees, opened the placket of Aiden's trousers and freed his stiff cock as a loud knock echoed through the house.

Aiden met his gaze. "Are you expecting company?"

He tucked Aiden's cock away. "Not at all." He listened as Finnegan attended the door, speaking gruffly to refuse the visitor entry.

A gentleman bellowed, "I'll see him right now, my good man. Bring me my son before I call the bloody watch on you."

CHAPTER THIRTEEN

Christ, not Lord Henderson. How had he found Terry? Aiden grasped his lover's hand. "What are you going to do?"

Terry shifted uncertainly on his feet, his glance alternating between the hall door and possible escape via the terrace door. He raised his finger to his lips to silence Aiden from asking further questions and pressed his ear to the door.

Although Aiden had proposed that Terry reveal his existence to his father just moments ago, he was not sure now was such a good time. Terry's face tightened with fury, the same expression that had utterly terrified Aiden for a moment when they had met in the dark of Covent Garden. He squeezed Terry's hand again to reassure himself that that frightening stranger was a fleeting aberration brought about only by extreme panic.

Terry turned his head, eyes hard and flat of emotion. He brushed his lips across Aiden's briefly, then turned the door handle and stepped out into the hall. "What's going on here?" he barked.

Surprised, Aiden followed.

Poor Finnegan was outmatched in size and determination against Henderson. The earl bristled with outrage, his skin a mottled red as he tried to reach his son.

Terry stood with his arms folded across his chest.

"Sorry, sir. This gentleman wants to see his son, but refuses to leave when I tell him there's no one here but you and His Grace."

"It is because of the duke that I am here, you fool. That man with him is my son."

Finnegan blinked comically. "Are you sure? He ain't no posh gentleman like you or His Grace."

Aiden stepped between Terry and his father. "Lord

Henderson, what a pleasant surprise."

"I bet you are." Henderson shook a fist. "Get out of my way or I will knock your block off. Your Grace," he added as an afterthought.

He sized him up. Henderson had a few extra pounds on him but was all fury. Aiden couldn't hope to stand against him without risk of injury. Perhaps he could talk their way out of this. As he opened his mouth to speak, though, Terry curled a hand over his shoulder and squeezed.

He gently nudged Aiden aside and stepped forward. "What is it you want, Lord Henderson?"

"My son and heir," Henderson growled.

Terry snorted. "Finnegan, if the children have woken from this racket take them outside to play for a time."

Lord Henderson started at the mention of children, his gaze flittering around the house in search of them. Finnegan shuffled toward the servants' quarters and the house fell silent.

Terry shrugged. "You have no son or heir in this house, my lord. I apologize for whoever misinformed you."

"Your face does not lie." Henderson approached. "Those are my eyes and my Emily's nose on your face."

"As I said before, your son is not here," Terrance said in a voice so quiet and deadly that Aiden began to worry he'd misjudged his lover's capacity for anger quite a bit.

Henderson stared, his jaw working. "Damn it, Terry. Where the devil have you been?"

"Nowhere fit for a child." His lover's expression grew guarded. "I am sorry for your loss, my lord, but the boy you are searching for is long gone. I think you should leave."

Henderson turned on Aiden. "You. What did you do to find him?"

Terry growled, "More than you damn well did."

Henderson's eyebrows rose. "I thought you dead."

"You thought?" A dry painful laugh spilled from Terry's mouth. "At least I take after my mother in terms of intellect. Did it not occur to you that you had the wrong child's body to bury?"

The earl's face fell. "I had neither you nor your mother to mourn over. The crypts at Edenmore are empty."

Terry shook his head. "And that did not stop you from marrying that harpy before a mere six months had passed after the accident. You allowed that woman to destroy Mother's pride and joy by letting her redecorate Henderson House," Terry hissed. "I'm surprised she didn't paper over mother's portrait or destroy it."

Aiden settled a hand over Terry's arm as his voice rose to a shout. His lover covered it with his and breathed deeply.

"So, you do have the painting? Thank God."

Terry shook off Aiden's grip and towered over his father. "Why do you care? Return to your family, Lord Henderson. You have none here that want you."

Henderson's skin changed from mottled red to deathly pale and that couldn't be good.

"Terry, that is enough," Aiden warned. He caught Henderson's elbow and steered him into the library. The earl gasped for air as he sat. He closed his eyes and Aiden worried that he might never open them again. He turned but found Terry unmoved, arms rigid at his sides. Aiden rushed past, "Do you want Amelia to be as fatherless as you?"

He poked his head out into the hall. "Finnegan," he shouted. Two heads popped out from a nearby doorway. "Come quickly. Lord Henderson looks to be seizing."

Finnegan's wife bustled into the library and pressed her hands to Lord Henderson's brow, touched his hands, and then peered into his eyes. "Likely only mild shock, Your Grace. I'll get some cool compresses for his temper. He needs to be calm."

Easy to suggest, but not easy to arrange in this situation. Aiden pushed Terry into an armchair opposite his father. "Now, sit there and wipe the scowl off your face—unless you'd like to inherit today."

Terry tipped his head back and met his gaze, the corner of his lips lifting in a rueful smile. "I truly don't want that."

"Neither did I." Aiden returned the grin. "Be civil and have a drink with the earl. I'll pour."

The lack of words behind Aiden's back while he poured three drinks was stifling. He handed one to Terry, sat one by the still puffing Lord Henderson, and settled himself to act as chaperone.

Henderson's eyes fluttered open. "Saw you last night and four years ago at another ball. Your hair was shorter then, clothes not so fine, but it was *you* flirting with my daughter."

Terry crossed his arms over his chest. "A decent man does not flirt with a half-sister. I did not speak to her last night."

"What did you want with her then?" The earl licked his lips. "To ruin her chances of making a match?"

Aiden snorted. "Did she have a full drawing room of gentlemen callers today? If so, it was entirely her brother's doing."

The earl shook his head. "It was your attentions last night that spurred the other gentlemen to step forward. The house has been smothered in flowers since first light."

He chuckled. "I danced with Lady Amelia at Terry's request. He was particularly distressed to have Lord Danbury anywhere near her and I was more than happy to oblige him with a favor."

Henderson stared at his son. "Why haven't you come home?"

"I've been home, as you call it, eight times." Terry crossed his leg over his knee. "There's no place for me there."

"Yes, there is." Henderson sat forward. "My second wife and daughters will just have to give way."

Aiden lifted his hands to stop the argument that looked to be moments away. "Gentlemen, perhaps this discussion is best left for another day when you are both cooler in temperament."

Terry shook his head. "We leave tomorrow."

Aiden closed his eyes as Lord Henderson spluttered, "You are not going anywhere, young man."

At the rate they were going, Henderson would truly have a seizure from the stress. When he opened them, Terry had stood, hands clenched into tight fists.

"Enough," Terrance shouted as he stormed out of the chamber, leaving Aiden alone with Lord Henderson.

The aggravated man made to follow his son, but Aiden pushed him down into his chair again. "Relax, my lord, he'll be back eventually."

"How can you be so sure?"

Finnegan's wife bustled in with a damp cloth and pressed it over the spluttering lord's head. "We'll keep this on 'till it heats then rinse it again in cool water."

Since that didn't sound too difficult for him to manage, Aiden caught her eye and tipped his head toward the door. "I'll call you should we need you again."

Although she frowned, she left as Aiden asked.

"Is it true?" Henderson asked suddenly.

"That Terry is leaving London? Yes, most definitely."

Henderson moaned. "I cannot lose him again. I've wondered about my boy all these years. We used to be very close. You have to convince him to remain."

No wonder Terry was so bitter about Henderson remarrying so swiftly and having a new family to replace him. But it was a child's reaction to disappointment to stomp and pout the way he did today. Eventually, Terry would calm down, but only if given enough time. "I cannot do that, my lord. He is determined to explore the Continent. If it is any consolation he will not be traveling alone. He has the children and will have my company, as well. He will not do anything foolish I promise you."

Henderson glared. "But will he come back?"

That decision would be entirely up to Terrance to make. Whatever he decided, however, would be good enough for Aiden. "I cannot make any promises on that head. If he does wish to return I will do everything in my power to smooth his way back into society."

The earl peered at him, his expression softening to puzzlement. "Why would you help him? He's nothing to you."

He grinned at the depths of his entanglement. Life

wasn't worth living without Terry in it. "He is my friend, even before I knew he was your heir."

"I will acknowledge his existence from today," Henderson stubbornly insisted. "I will let everyone know that Viscount Hathaway is alive and well. I'll hold a dinner this very week."

Oh, good God, did Henderson not listen to a word spoken to him? Terry wasn't ready for that kind of introduction. What if one of the guests was a prior customer? He shuddered. "Lord Henderson, while I do not know the particulars in detail, your son suffered terribly at the hands of others after the accident that took his mother. Things no child should experience, he says. Do not push him into society like this or I fear you will never see him again. He's done it easily before of his own free will."

The earl pulled the cloth from his head. His color was much better and his chest no longer heaved. "If he will not change his mind, will you write me of his whereabouts? Can you work on changing his mind? He must inherit."

Reluctantly, Aiden nodded. A few years on the Continent might change his mind. "We will see."

Henderson dragged himself out of the chair and held out his hand. "Don't take too long, I'm not getting any younger."

❧

Despite the racket Maggie and Gerard were making across the garden, Terrance heard Aiden's approach.

"He's gone now," the duke murmured.

"Good." *Damn good of the old man to get the hell away from him.* Terrance hadn't liked conversing with his father.

Aiden's fingers brushed his thigh. "He's resigned himself to your plans for travel and insists one of us write him."

Terrance raked his fingers through his hair. He wouldn't be writing to anyone but Henry. "What is it with people and letters?"

Aiden's shrug jostled his shoulder. "Makes them happy to hear from us, as I understand it. It isn't too big an imposition, is it?"

Gerard and Maggie raced around them, spinning happily as if they had always lived here. When they moved away to pester Finnegan, Terrance sighed. "You think I should claim my title and position in society, don't you?"

His lover leaned hard against his side. "I think you should not rush to make a decision one way or another. As Viscount Hathaway, you would have wealth and comfort. A half-sister who needs you. A friend who would like his friendship acknowledged as far as society needs to know. There are many things here in London we could enjoy together."

Terrance curled an arm around Aiden's back for a quick hug. "Do you know you smile as you talk now? You used to be so serious and stern."

Aiden's lips curved into a smile as he focused on the children darting about the garden beds and squealing. "That was before I met the real you. I am disgustingly giddy with joy. I barely recognize myself."

"Giddy, eh?" Terry leaned closer. "There is this position I have heard of, requiring one partner to be hung upside down while his balls and arse are licked. Want to try it tonight? There will be little chance for pleasure once onboard ship."

Aiden's breath caught. "As long as you are with me, I'm up for anything. Will you think me a fool if I tell you I'm in love with you?"

Terrance gasped. He'd never expected so much from Aiden. He was glad he'd taken a chance on the dark and dangerous Duke of Lewes. Like him, he had hidden layers, the greatest one—his stubborn, fragile heart. He twined his fingers through his lover's and squeezed. "You say the most extraordinary things, Your Grace, that my heart cannot take much more."

The duke's smile was as warm as the sunset. "Then take me, any which way you choose."

Lust, an ever present hunger, stirred within him. "Don't think I won't bend you over, Aiden Banks, at the slightest provocation. By God, I'm itching for it."

"Then have at it." He tugged Terrance toward the house, a sinfully wicked glint in his eyes as the sun set on the first day of their adventure together.

EPILOGUE

Terry stood stiffly at the ship's railing, gaze fixed on the docks as they drew closer. "Think he will be there?"

Aiden scanned the crowd. "Have you ever known him to miss a potentially emotional reunion?"

"Gentlemen do not weep," Gerard, now ten, insisted as he bounced up and down in excitement.

Today the boy began his own adventure. Today he became Terry's legal son in the eyes of polite society—a lie so elaborate Aiden had goggled at Staines' proposal sent a year ago, a month after they had left London. Guilt had worked on Staines' mind at the part he'd played in Terry's life. Over the past year, Staines had cajoled, bribed and threatened murder to provide Terry with a plausible history after the accident that took his mother's life—a lie good enough to pass the *ton's* intense scrutiny including an early marriage, two children, and flight to the Continent to avoid his overwhelming debts.

Those imaginary debts were paid now and as far as the *ton* believed, Aiden was bringing him home.

"Ladies surely do cry a lot," Maggie argued. "My governess was always weeping over some trifling matter."

Aiden lifted her into his arms so she could see the crowd better. Although Maggie insisted she was too grown up to allow it often, she curled her arms about his neck tightly in excitement. "Maggie, my girl, you are about to see an extraordinary event. The Duke of Staines is about to cry like a baby when he sees us." He tickled her cheek and she giggled.

"You are so silly, Aiden."

"And you, my girl, are a delight. See there, my sister-in-law, Mrs. Banks, is waiting to escort us home to London. She will likely boss you around mercilessly, as she does with everyone in the house, but she has our best interests at heart. She wrote to say she's looking forward to meeting you and has fixed up your bed chamber at Mercer House very prettily."

Maggie wriggled to get down and smoothed her skirts as her French governess had taught her and arranged her face into a genteel smile. "That was very kind of her."

Aiden snorted and met Terry's gaze. He appeared uncertain and Aiden leaned against his side, brushing his knuckles along his thigh as if by accident. "Your father is here, so is Amelia."

He swallowed and his chin dipped the smallest amount. Clearly he still had doubts about this homecoming. "I see them."

Terry had taken over Aiden's correspondence to Lord Henderson after six months and the two appeared friendly, at least on paper. The earl hadn't been happy that Terry wouldn't reside under his roof, but there was little he could do to change the situation since Aiden refused to retract his invitation. "We'll be at Mercer House soon. I'm looking forward to unpacking for good this time."

While the trip had been exceptional, Aiden had missed the comforts of his home. He'd even missed Josephine and Robert. He'd never thought to admit that. But life had changed for the better when Terrance had returned to him. He'd learned to trust, to let someone care for him and care for them in return.

The children ran toward the prow as the ship was tied securely to the docks.

Terry dug into his pocket, produced a key, and twirled it in his fingers. "Do you think we should open that locked chest of yours when we get home, Your Grace? I'm curious to discover as to what it contains."

Aiden gulped. "I thought you'd thrown that key away long ago."

A sinful smile twisted Terry's mouth. "Now, Your Grace, how could I do that to you? After all, you followed me halfway 'round the world and received little recompense. Surely, I can make your sacrifice worth the wait." He dropped the key into his pocket and patted it. "I've made extensive plans for the contents of that chest.

Be ready."

Ready? Aiden thought he might explode here and now. They'd had little opportunity for extended bed play while they traveled, and none at all while onboard ship. He ached to be touched and fucked hard and fast by his lover. He had to wait now 'till they were secure in his home.

But what would Terry say when he discovered not a chest but an entire chamber suited to Aiden's form of pleasure? A collection so vast it would take months to experiment with all the devices he'd locked away.

His lover joined his children at the prow, pointing to those gathered on the docks with a grin.

Aiden wrestled his raging lust back under control, even while marveling that his tender-hearted partner intended to dominate him the first chance he got. He may claim not to be his master now, but Terry's whim controlled him as surely as he'd wielded a whip long ago.

Terry waved at Aiden to join them where he stood with his children clustered about him. Pulse thrumming, body aching, he rushed toward the man who'd turned his world upside down and back to rights again.

Life was infinitely better than he'd imagined it could be.

He knew where he belonged and what to do. He knew what it meant to love.

THE END

ABOUT THE AUTHOR

Bestselling historical author Heather Boyd believes every character she creates deserves their own happily-ever-after, no matter how much trouble she puts them through. With that goal in mind, she weaves sizzling English set love stories that push the boundaries of regency era propriety to keep readers enthralled until the wee hours of the morning. Brimming with new ideas, she frequently wishes she could type as fast as she conjures new storylines. While writing full time north of Sydney, Australia, Heather collects dust bunnies in all corners of the house and does her best to wrangle her testosterone-fuelled family into submission.

For more information visit
www.heather-boyd.com

ALSO BY HEATHER BOYD

The Distinguished Rogues Series:
Chills
Broken
Charity
An Accidental Affair
Keepsake
An Improper Proposal
Reason to Wed
The Trouble with Love
Married by Moonlight

The Wild Randalls Series:
Engaging the Enemy
Forsaking the Prize
Guarding the Spoils
Hunting the Hero

Miss Mayhem Series:
Miss Watson's First Scandal
Miss George's Second Chance
Miss Radley's Third Dare

Short Stories:
One Wicked Night
Wicked Mourning
In the Widow's Bed
Love Me Tender
Love Me True
The Almack's Alternative
A Husband for Mary

The Hunt Club Series

BOOK 1, ALMOST AN EQUAL

When the Duke of Byworth's empty marriage is threatened by a fellow duke he is naturally aggrieved. Nathan cannot allow the potentially damaging contents of his wife's diary to reveal the depths of their estrangement because exposure of his secret dalliances with other men would taint his innocent children's lives. Not to mention end his life. So, without revealing his mission to his steward, Henry Stackpool, a man he trusts for everything else, Nathan undertakes to steal the diary back alone.

Former pickpocket and molly house whore, Henry Stackpool, works hard to keep his position as right hand to a moral man, the Duke of Byworth, but he fears his kind hearted employer is ill-equipped for a confrontation with his unstable opponent. Henry cannot explain the source of his knowledge without exposing the secrets of his past. So when fate places Henry in harm's way, he risks his hard won reputation and freedom to retrieve the duchess's diary himself.

BOOK 3 HARDLY A STRANGER

The Duke of Staines has the worst luck in wives and lovers. A widow for fifteen years, Ambrose is busy running his gentleman's club, snatches pleasure from transient lovers, and relies on Francis Redding to provide intelligent companionship between social engagements. There is only one problem with his relationship with Redding; the man would make the perfect lover, if only he wasn't a dependant servant.

Life-long footman to the Duke of Staines, Francis Redding, is hardly a stranger to the disappointment of unreachable dreams or the duke's unorthodox love life. He's lived in the duke's shadow for most of his life, trained as a surgeon at his request, too, and has all too frequently kept the duke out of trouble. It's not a bad life for a farmer's son, until the duke's luck runs out.

On the surface, Raphael has everything he needs: good friends, a title, and membership to the decadent Hunt Club where forbidden pleasure can be had at a moments notice. Pretending is not what he wants. Expectations by family and friends keep his feelings for Lord Claymore at bay. When his best friend returns to London in a black mood, Rafe sets out to cheer him up and make Claymore's upcoming birthday an event to remember.

Shaken and uneasy of his growing attraction to men, James has reached an uncomfortable crossroads in his well-ordered, respectable life. Plans to end his torment on his birthday are mere days away. However, his intention to explore forbidden passion just once comes unstuck. Can James follow through with his well-reasoned, sensible decision when a man who knows what he wants, needs him too?

Victor Knight has never been able to juggle his work and love life to anyone's satisfaction. A hardworking investment banker in London, he's obsessed with maintaining his clients' privacy and profits, and cannot understand why those same clients are withdrawing funds when he's making them a good profit. When a dull evening supper at the Hunt Club ends in a blunt invitation to have sex with the Earl of Beecroft, he welcomes the distraction on the proviso they never discuss his business affairs.

Daniel Wellham, the Earl of Beecroft, has long admired Victor Knight. He even understands and admires the banker's preoccupation with work. Their night together is everything he hoped it would be and while he longs for permanence, his secret life as a spy means he can never reveal too much of his own history. Unfortunately, when he realizes that all is not right in Victor's life, those promises he made to keep his nose out of the banker's business means he cannot offer to help or explain that his latest mission might take him away forever. How can love and trust be possible when duty and responsibility prevent total honesty?